WHAT
LOVE

OTHER BOOKS BY
BLUE MOON AUTHORS

Anonymous
Souvenirs from a
Boarding School

Denise Hall
A Brief Education

Edith Cadivec
Eros: The Meaning
of My Life

Jac Lenders
Excess of Love

David (Sunset) Carson
Lament

Richard Manton
Max

**Gerald and Caroline
Greene**
S-M: The Last Taboo

Alexander Trocchi
Helen and Desire

To order or
for a full catalogue,
contact:

BLUE MOON BOOKS
61 FOURTH AVE.
NEW YORK, NY 10003
Phone: (212) 505-6880
Fax: (212) 673-1039

New Tempo

WHAT LOVE

Maria Madison

BLUE MOON
BLUE MOON BOOKS, INC. NEW YORK

What Love
ISBN 0-929654-86-2
CIP data available from the Library of Congress

Manufactured in the United States of America
Published by Blue Moon Books, Inc.
61 Fourth Avenue
New York, NY 10003

Cover design by Steve Brower

WHAT
LOVE

1.

I'm waiting at the bus stop. The video films in my bag are due back at the shop before 7:30. I'm late, and so is the bus. I consider walking to the next stop, looking over my shoulder every five seconds in case it comes in sight up the hill before the roundabout. I never do like waiting. Wasted time is futile. It makes me itch. Nothing constructive ever happens at bus stops, although there's plenty of time to think. But I don't want to do that just now. I want to keep on moving, to feel I'm doing something and that even in the simplest actions there's a purpose. Might the minutiae of life all join up somewhere into a kind of whole where it all makes sense? A framework, a justification for living? Yes, I know divorce affects people like this but I never thought it would happen to me. And here I am, chasing the little things, not giving the past a chance to slip into my mind and foul it all up.

It's autumn, the time of year I like best. It suits me. I like the way the sunlight melts everything with a glow like butter. It all looks kinder. More worn and relaxed. Summer raises people's expectations too much. They go crazy, pouring out of the city in their cars only to sweat in jams and find the countryside worn and polluted. But you can relax into autumn. It's such a gentle let down, like a tire with a slow puncture. You can flow with it, ebb away.

Spring's nice too, but so fierce once it gets going. There's no subtlety. All the blossom shouts in sorbet colors. The energy bursts above ground and doesn't care how loud or how fast it is. It's hard to keep pace. I've heard the time from mid-February to the end of April is the worst time for nervous breakdowns. I suppose all the energy from the earth coming to life again disturbs the brain. It's like we're too delicate, unable to cope with the surge of the equinox, so it rips right through us and we get lost in its force. I ought to know about that, but I don't like to think. I almost went under myself only a few months ago.

No, autumn suits me. My birthday's in September. Maybe that's why in a curious way, I identify with these short months, although it's a season when all visible nature is slowly dying—I don't know.

Birthday or not, I don't suppose I'll be celebrating. I'll be back at college then, trying to do my job, trying not to wince when we pass in the corridor. I'd like to change my job. I don't want this continual confrontation with pain.

8

The bus is late. I check my watch but it's no help. Four minutes slow, always. I'm the only person waiting underneath the shade of the massive beech as the brown leaves spin down around me. The cars pull away fast from the roundabout, mostly one man per car. Men in suits. Executives. The later they come home, the more well-paid the job. I notice the way they look at me as they drive past, tugging their ties. I don't feel comfortable the way I'm dressed: old jeans, old lilac jumper with some of the beaded embroidery around the neck missing. Worn wooden sandals on my feet. And on each toe, the pink nail polish is chipped. It reminds me of the party I didn't go to last week because I lost my nerve. A guilty reproach each time I look down.

My face is a mess too. I'm not wearing my usual makeup, my mask. I can't look at these men in their cars. I've nothing to hide behind, though I suppose it wouldn't make much odds if my foundation was perfect, the blusher in the right place and not a garish streak across my cheeks. In truth, I haven't been able to meet eyes with a man for a long time. It's only recently I've gone back to lining my eyes. I cried too much in February. It made them look worse.

So I'm standing here, my face naked, feeling awkward, waiting for a bus. I feel like a schoolgirl, a teenager, and it's awful. I know if someone honks at me (even though I've read women don't blush at thirty) I'll go red and my mouth will tighten like a zip. The next few minutes will be

9

spent trying to relax. I know the soles of my feet will sweat and the smooth wooden surface of my sandals will get slippery. I'll lose a clog boarding the bus. And so it goes on.

The leaves of the big old beech make a crispy rustling sound as the wind blows through. I look up. Trees are magnificent. I've always loved them. When I was a little girl my father made a swing for me in an old oak. I walked across a field of buttercups and cows to sit on the short, worn plank of wood, and grip the rusty chains either side. I'd throw my head back and watch the heavy branches overhead flying through the sky. The chains became smooth in time, under my child's tight grasp. Even now I remember clearly how they felt, how it all looked. Clutching the canvas bag with the videos I feel tears coming, popping over my lower lids, running down my cheeks. I can't cry here, at the bus stop with all the estate agents, solicitors and managers flitting by me, their eyes flickering as they pass. It's ridiculous. Embarrassing. A woman crying in the street. And what are these unbidden, inappropriate tears for? Memories? The innocence of childhood lost? February? Just me, in a moment's unguarded self pity? I don't know. But they come a lot lately. I don't seem to have feelings at the moment, only tears. The feelings have gone as if someone has taken them from me and walked off with them in a bag. I must find this person and reclaim them. That's how it is. Numb. Bloody hopeless.

I don't notice the man at first. He's standing about ten yards away, close into the wall. When

I see him, he's like a shadow, not really there in the flesh. A phantom in a heavy coat leaning back into the autumn twilight. I dash the wetness from my face. God! He may have been there for some time watching me. Seeing me cry. I take a couple of steps toward him. He's looking at Denwood Court, a small select block of flats set in the middle of an immaculate barbered lawn. He gives no sign he's noticed me at all. Perhaps he's just come from there and slipped across the grass at the side. That way, I would have missed him. I look up at the windows expecting to see someone looking down. A woman waving perhaps? But I don't see a soul looking out.

He turns on his heels and pieces of gravel crunch under his shoes as he comes out of the shade. He walks very slowly up to me, swinging his body slightly, hands stuffed deep into the pockets of his coat. A controlled walk. Very cool. Something about it makes me shrink inside as if those few paces are a prelude to future intimacy. A blush creeps up my face. I ought to keep my fantasies more under wraps.

I haven't been able to look a man in the eye since around February. I think a lot about what it would be like to have those flirty sensual messages going again. I guess now I couldn't cope with any kind of sexual signalling. I'd give too much away. So when he speaks, I find myself staring red-faced at his shoes.

I can tell a man's character by his shoes. The leather and style are the best c.v. there is. His shoes are beautiful: pale-grey leather with a lambskin tongue, a tiny leather twist going over it. Stemar Italian. About a hundred and sixty pounds. How do I know? I do. I shop all the time for imaginary boyfriends. The feel of fine wool excites me—the feel of knife-creases in the trousers. He has neat feet, I notice that.

'I should be soon.' I admire his shoes and smile shyly as though his face shone in them. I wish it did. I'd have the courage to stare at it then. Pretty soon I'll have a collection of males I won't recognize unless they're wearing shoes.

He sighs and walks away and the leather heels tap on the pavement. Now I can stare at his back. Already he's wearing a coat, and it's only the beginning of autumn. A fine wool herringbone with a black velvet collar. Three buttons on the cuff. The cut is impeccable. While I stare he turns and smiles briefly at me.

'I don't usually go by bus.'

Of course you don't. Men like you never do. You should have a Porsche waiting outside your office. You'll ruin your coat sitting in public transport. They never clean the seats. Buses always stink of semi-continent old ladies. The stink gets worse in the rain. You should have taken a taxi.

'I think they may have missed one out.'

'Just my luck.'

A grin then. It knocks me off balance. I catch a flash of teeth, a glint in his eye but I can't retain the rest of his face. If he were blind—God forbid!—I'd be able to pore over every centimeter. I can't do that while he's looking at me.

The beech seems suddenly fascinating. I look

up and feel the flush stretch down my neck. My throat is a vulnerable spot and he's looking at it. I know he is.

The leaves sound like paper decorations rustling in a draught. They are fired around the edges with orange, little clusters of orange, batting in the breeze. They remind me of many failed attempts to make origami butterflies for the Christmas tree. Trees, the largest and longest-lived beings on our planet. Silent maintainers of life. I look up at the trunk and the ascending branches, the heartwood poised in prayer. Silent witness to so much. Me, so small beneath. Unable to regulate my own life.

I have a picture on my bedroom wall I tore from a book and had framed. The whole page is black with hazy shapes in the center foreground. Above is a tree of lightning. Thin white lines make up the branches and meet at a point where they become the trunk, discharging to earth in one great white thigh of fire. I like the picture in the kind of pessimistic way I find comforting. Life, it says, is nothing but shuddering molecules. The force of creation and destruction is the same. The tree grows up—the lightning cuts it down. It is almost the law of things, to be destroyed in their prime.

Somehow, because I no longer feel inferior and frightened, only small, I can look at the man's face because he's small too, compared with the beautiful arrogance of the beech.

Good-looking men never seem to stay in my head. I can study their faces for as long as I'm able, but later when I try to recall the details, I can't. I need a snapshot to give me a mental in-

13

ventory, which I must keep looking at. Take it away and I can remember very little. Why, I ask myself? Perhaps it's something to do with the way I desire beauty, how lustfully I see it in men. Like Dali said, *'La beauté n'est que la somme de conscience de nos perversions.'* I tend to see men through my fantasies of which I'm sometimes ashamed. I can't, it seems, see them objectively. I'm too possessive and it clouds the memory. If you want something, walk away from it. Turn, and it's yours. I desire too much and it always eludes me. Later, too soon, these men become only a disappointing blur, a lost feeling.

He's good-looking. Enough to make you hurt. He has tight dark curls, slight curls, slightly longer in the nape so their darkness meets the blackness of his collar. His mouth is wide, well-shaped, with a mocking lift at the corners. Half a smile sits on his lips. His eyes are intense, dark. They are not deep-set but have the appearance of being so, because the olive tint of his skin around them creates a shadow. As I catalogue, he takes off his coat and flicks it over his arm. The suit underneath is grey, pin-striped, with three buttons on the cuff like the coat.

'It's hot,' he says. 'Whew.'

Hidden by this neat, precise image is another man, I can sense it. Something unexpected, possibly fun, possibly dangerous, may jump out at any moment. The suit makes it lie down.

I consider for a moment walking to the next stop, but I can't. The bus will pass me before I get there and I'll look silly. He'll smile indulgently at my impatience and I'll turn at that moment as I walk along to catch the amused gleam in his eyes as he looks at me from the bus. I'll stay here, uncomfortable as I am. I'm stuck with him.

I sigh. 'I have to return some videos before the place closes,' I say boldly.

He comes back to me from his pacing up and down. 'People should complain,' he says, but the smile in his eyes tells me he doesn't mean it. He's not bothered by a late bus, I can see that. He wants to test me, tease a little.

'Maybe it's broken down.'

'There should be another on stand-by.'

The smile is confusingly ever-present. I shuffle around the confines of two pavement slabs thinking what to say next. He cuts into my thought, talking to the back of my neck, his voice a purr. Am I going to the video library in R—? I nod. Very poor selection, he says. Mostly kids stuff. I feel he's insulting me, or am I being silly? I tell him I had to watch some films for college next week to help me prepare for a lesson. I sound shamefully defensive.

'You're a teacher?'

'Only part-time.'

He laughs and I feel both annoyed and flattered by the sound. My body temperature seems to have risen significantly.

'You don't look the part,' he says, still laughing.

I know him. He's one of those people who can make me laugh when I'm quite furious. I had an uncle who could charm me out of a mood when I was a child. Don't smile or your face will crack,

15

he'd say, defying me not to, playing with my emotions. And when my lips ungraciously twisted into a smile I did not feel, I hated him.

But to my surprise, a genuine laugh bubbles up from my throat.

'Why do you say that?'

'You don't look tough enough. I can't imagine you and a class of loutish sixteen-year-olds.'

'I cope. Perfectly well.'

'You shouldn't.'

'And why?'

There is a pause while he turns away and holds his breath for a second as if he's about to deliver a verdict. 'You're too delicate.'

Well! This good-looking man is a total stranger! I've never seen him around here before! He speaks to me as if he knows me, or knows something about me. Perhaps he's a friend of Zack. No— Zack's friends are mainly lecturers like himself. This guy is too smooth, too self-contained, too clever for his taste. Still, since February I've met some weird people I never would have wanted to know when I was married. So why not the same for Zack? Perhaps his circle of friends has changed, widened. Impulsively, I ask.

'Are you a friend of my ex? Zack F—?'

His eyebrows rise slowly and he smiles. There's a pause before he speaks and I realize this is a habit. 'I don't think I am. Zack F—? Your husband?'

I look down at his shoes. 'My ex-husband. I thought you might know him.'

The pause. 'Why?' he says, clicking his tongue,

'Because you think I'm being too familiar with you?'

I laugh awkwardly. 'Of course not.'

There is a low wall running along the inside edge of the pavement. Suddenly he jumps up and onto the lawn belonging to the block of flats. He walks to the trunk of the old beech and runs his hands over the bark. He talks to himself as he circles the tree. It's a poem.

'. . . that thou, light-winged Dryad of the trees,
In some melodious plot
of beechen green, and shadows numberless
Singest of autumn in full-throated ease.'

He comes back across the grass, jumps onto the pavement and walks toward me, dusting his hands.

'Keats, isn't it?' I say.

The smile twitches slightly. 'Ode to a. . . .'

'Nightingale.'

'Spot the deliberate mistake?'

I frown. 'No.'

He swirls on his heels. 'Wrong season.'

'Oh.'

At that moment the blue and buff shape of the bus comes slowly up the hill to the roundabout. I feel as though someone has stolen a cream cake from under my nose. The world seems without promise.

'. . . of beechen green, and shadows numberless,
Singest of summer in full-throated ease,' he says, giving me the correct version.

'Oh,' I say, 'Yes.'

He does not step back for me to board the bus,

17

but jumps on the platform with me, he on one side, I on the other. He goes downstairs, sliding into the first seat. I go to the upper deck where it's cooler. The open windows at the front blow the smells away. If I sit third from the front I'll get a warm breeze in my face. It may bring me to my senses.

Half a mile further on he gets off and walks briskly away to a staggered block of exclusive maisonettes, fronted by a copse of birches. His neighbors on either side would be big people. Very big, in their massive houses with gardens like fields.

I fancy he looks back and up at me sitting by the window, but he doesn't really. He half turns to wave to a car that hoots as it turns down a side road, but he's forgotten me. When I'm sure he's not going to look back, I let my eyes stare at him indecently. If you can't have someone, the imaginative possibilities have to be the next best thing.

At the video hire shop in R— the world seems coarser. The place is full of teenage boys eyeing the top shelf. Here, there are large red stickers saying 'OUT' on the cases. 'Secrets of a Night Nurse' is OUT. So is 'Confessions of a Sex Slave.' OUT. The youths topple the boxes from the shelves and look dispassionately at the stills on the covers. They've seen them all before, but still study them moodily. I hand in the two vidoes I've been watching in preparation for next week and turn to go. On the way out I catch sight of

18

an old favorite. Pushing through the line of young men with their elbows on the counter I hand over the membership card and £1.50. It's been a long time since I've seen this one, 'The Postman Always Rings Twice.'

2.

I live in a part of the city which frightens most people. I see it in their faces. When I had to leave my address for delivery of a chair two weeks ago, I saw the saleswoman's eyes widen. You don't live *there* she might well have said.

I've been here for seven years and never had any trouble. There was a riot here two years ago, it's true, but about half a mile down the road, not on my doorstep. My mother rang me the morning after to see if I was all right. I had heard nothing. Nothing at all. The news coverage was awful: blacks torching, looting, attacking the police. I tried to get Zack to come with me and have a look at the damage. He wouldn't. He told me I was one of those people who drive to the scene of a crash for vicarious entertainment after Sunday lunch. It wasn't like that for me at all. I feel part of this place. It's my home. The young blacks come to the college. They're okay.

I left Zack, dressed in old clothes and went to the riot zone. There were crowds, silent and waiting, on the streets. I talked to some people I knew. I wanted to find out what really happened—I never believe what's printed in the papers. The police lined up across the road with their riot shields in front of them. It was tempting to want to throw a brick or a can at their stony, unforgiving faces. It gave me the shivers and I came home. Zack told me I was crazy. He didn't want to know what I'd seen or heard.

Apart from that time two years ago, we have had little trouble here—at least on the surface. But people who come here from the South are spooked by all the colored faces. The old imperialism comes out. They look at each black as though he's about to steal their job, or steal something. They don't care much for Asians either. One of my neighbors had a little boy who was run over by a car and killed at the bottom of our road. When his coffin was carried out of the house five days later, some of the white women in our street came out to watch. They stood in their aprons, leaning on brooms and smoking, among the mourners. They feel it differently from us, one said. It's their religion. They don't let these kind of events bother them. I shall never forget what I saw. I've never seen so many men cry so openly. Tears on brown faces. Unlike me they can let out their emotions.

In Victorian times this district was well-off, genteel. Then they sculpted the neighborhood park

21

and boating lake. There was a boathouse, punts on the lake. It's all gone now.

In the South there are miles of identical houses, great chunks of semis. Narrow-minded people, all the same, the crass mass consciousness going with their environment. It's different here. Streets, houses within streets are so unalike. It's as though the area was built piecemeal; a few 1910 terraced houses, then large seedy mansions with adjoining coach houses, all white pillars and huge sash windows, falling to pieces.

Zack and I lived in this house, a post-war semi with large garden built in the thirties. It still has the original leaded windows, some with colored glass. We could have lived half a mile along the road to R— in a lah-de-dah detached house. But Zack's a left winger. He teaches at the college. He couldn't have his black students find out we had material aspirations, so we had to live here. We have Sikh neighbors on one side, and an Afro-Caribbean family with four children on the other.

In February, when Zack went, he said I could have the house. There wasn't any fuss. He even had a preliminary agreement drawn up by his solicitor before the divorce. He knew after seven years everything would have to be split down the middle. As it was he left me all of it, using his money to set up house with his new woman, on the other—more expensive—side of the city. So much for his altruism.

Five large detached places are opposite my house. When Zack and I moved in they were empty and boarded up. The council was planning to demolish them in order to widen the road. It dragged on for years. I even added my bit about the trees.

There are five trees, two limes and three beeches on a grass slope outside our house. They have been there for over half a century. If the road was widened, they would have to come down. I hate people who cut down part of the life-force on our planet. When the council men came to take measurements I got really angry. I won't let them do it, I said. I'll climb high in any one of those trees and throw down the ladder. I'll get others on my side. We'll cause a lot of trouble.

As it turned out the scheme was scrapped. The trees are still there—for the moment.

Last week a Vietnamese family moved into one of those houses. They don't speak English. I keep trying to count how many of them there are. I haven't managed it yet although I did see ten going in the other night.

Next to them the house with the yellow windows is empty. Grass and weeds in the driveway are as high as an uncut field. Nobody wants to live there. Last year the woman who did was murdered by her lover. Let out of prison, he came back at six in the morning with an axe. He chopped through the front door and went up to the bedroom where he attacked her. I heard the screams of the man she had been in bed with. I heard the screams of her kids. Finally her screams, and then the silence. I saw the police arrive and run out. By the time reinforcements arrived he had cut her to pieces. I saw her come out on a

23

stretcher, under a blanket, all blood, all falling apart. It made me feel sick. Zack and I moved our bedroom to the one at the back of the house. It was bad seeing the rubber-gloved men carrying out stained furnishings over the next few weeks. I heard a short time ago the place had been bought by a local housing association. Mercedes, my black neighbor told me she had spoken to the workmen who came in to redecorate. They couldn't paint over the faint stains on the wall. They were spooked, she said. They didn't want the job.

I've grown used to looking at the peeling paint-work and those sad windows by now. I've imagined what happened inside so often, it ceases to terrify me like it used to. I've had to cope, being on my own.

After Zack left, I went mad, decorating. Every-thing had to be green. It became an obsession. I bought jungle wallpaper with elephants on it and papered the living room. I did all the paintwork dark green. I filled all the window sills with plants and stood tall ones in front of the French windows where they grew like trees. I bought dried larkspur and statice, and collected grasses to fill earthen-ware pots. I wanted it all full, luxuriant, bursting, the green and the flowers tumbling all over the house, which felt so empty.

Zack came over one afternoon and gave me a present: a framed print of 'Boer War.' There she is now, the dark lady, with her fingers to her lips, wondering what to do next. If he'd given it to me before February, I'd have called it prophetic.

If someone's going to leave you, I guess February's not such a bad time to go. The lighter evenings make people more optimistic—even abandoned women like me. I don't think I could have coped if Zack had gone before Christmas, say in November, because spring seems years away then and I hate winter. But if I'd known he'd been screwing Carol over the Christmas holiday, I doubt if I would have minded. I never found out till afterwards.

Zack left me because he said we'd grown apart. They all say that, don't they? What he really meant was that I wasn't interested in his ego any more, and he'd met a younger flibbert who was. He was right though. I had lost interest. Especially in sex.

He was one of those men who pretend they don't like sex because the animal part of them emerges and they don't know how to cope with it. He's a considerate lover. He has a set procedure from which he never departs. I shouldn't be surprised if he hasn't written it down somewhere in a book. I know when he wanted me because he always brushed his teeth beforehand as if some faint odor hung on his breath and might offend. His expression never altered either before, during, or for about an hour afterwards. Once, at a political demonstration when he was asked to speak I saw that same face. Serious, flushed, and vaguely uncomfortable.

There must always be something to distract him. He would kiss me with his eyes open, as if pleading for something to arrest his vision, so as to draw his mind away from what he was doing.

25

Once I found him engrossed in a cauliflower on the table behind me. Well, at least I can find some humor in the situation. I used to feel mad when I thought of him sharing all that he shared with me, with a flibbert.

My feelings about sex since then have been mainly based on self-deception. I tell myself I don't want it because it wasn't that wonderful with Zack. I tell myself I'm an easy celibate. Yes, yes, I know. But the truth is, I don't know how to go about sex now, without getting hurt. I don't want to go crazy like you're supposed to after divorce. That's a cliché. I don't want to go to bed with just anyone, simply to feed my ego, to feel somebody out there still fancies me.

I think it's been good for me on my own. I've sorted a few things out. When Zack fucked me something was missing. I know it now, but I still can't work out what it is. I need the man who holds the key to this forbidden door I'm faintly aware of, yet terrified to open by myself. I don't suppose he exists.

Zoe and Midge and Holly at the support group were very good to me after the breakup. It's been the first time I've really had the time to get to know them as people. Marriage kind of swallows you up. Holly encouraged me to put an advertisement in a respectable contact magazine—the one which looks for life partners rather than a blind screw. I haven't had any replies yet. It takes months for your ad to appear. I could have found someone during that time—or walked under a bus.

3.

The week before college it's hot. Too hot to go back and be mausoleumed in the shabby brick walls. Now, after the lousy summer, the weather decides to change and it's too late. The kids are all back at school. Next week the college students return.

I feel restless in the house. It's too hot to do any gardening which I usually do when I'm feeling uptight. I wish I had a car so I could drive out of the city into the country but Zack took it. I decide to walk to R— instead, not taking the bus. I'm curious about those maisonettes and the man at the bus stop. I can't seem to get him out of my head.

The day I came back from the video shop I went straight to the Keats anthology in my bookshelf. I checked the first stanza to 'Ode to a Nightingale.' I've never heard a nightingale sing. I've missed out. Who is this stranger who strokes the bark of trees, reciting poetry, bringing romance and magic

27

to lines learnt years ago at school? What kind of person does these things? He must be well-read, intellectual, not like the poet manqué's at college in the English department. Jealously, they hack every poem that comes their way to pieces.

It's Wednesday morning and I'm alone in the sun. The walk is pleasant. I move quickly away from the poor areas to the large houses set well back from the road. They all have oval rose beds edged with silver-grey catmint and blue clumps of fading lobelia flanking their gravel drives. It looks as though the same gardener has had his way with every frontage. I notice the burglar alarms, the anti-people alarms. All this wealth lying next-door to inner city poverty is obscene.

It's further than I think to the maisonettes and I'm sweating by the time I reach their cool, shady frontage and the birches, which make a small inviting copse in front of them. A narrow path runs through the slender trunks and I follow it, glad to get away from the heat of the pavement. It's quiet here. Lovely. Everyone appears to be out at work. I walk past the front doors, seeing closed windows. The sudden shout of music cuts through the silence and makes me turn and go slowly back. The music dies away as a window slams shut. Then I notice that the front door in the end ground-floor maisonette is wide open. There's a man in the doorway. He shouts 'Hi.' It's him. I feel I've been spying on him, chasing him like a schoolgirl with a crush. My innocent walk seems to be anything but innocent. The color rushes up my neck to my cheeks.

He walks toward me through a porch flanked by a large purple-flowered clematis climbing over a wooden trellis. I stand still, stupid in surprise with my mouth open.

Today there's no suit. He wears jeans and a white sleeveless tee shirt. He's not big, but there's stealth in those muscles. He has nothing on his feet. I blink, looking at them. He seems different without his shoes.

'Hi,' he says again. 'Like the Indian summer?'

The stammer I lost when I was thirteen comes back. 'It's a b-bit too hot to me.'

Pause. 'Really? The English always complain,' he smiles, lowers his head a little, 'don't we?'

I shrug. 'I suppose so.'

His thumbs drag on the belt loops at the front of his trousers, pulling them down slightly so the dark curl of hair below his navel is visible. I feel a sudden panic and want to run away, but he is talking, persuading.

'Fancy a cold drink? It's cooler inside,' he says.

'No. Really. I'm on my way now. I've got to—' I step back as the thumbs slide out from the belt and he extends one arm towards me.

'Come on. Don't be silly.'

Already his hand is in the small of my back guiding me to the open front door. I ask myself why I am going with a complete stranger. I must be crazy. But it's the timbre of his voice, a kind of do-as-you-will, do-as-you-won't quality about it. A soft voice, yet very clear, where emotions just scratch the surface. A voice from a man who doesn't care if I don't go with him because he's absolutely sure I will. He must read my subconscious, not listen to the rubbish coming from my mouth.

Inside, the cool white of the hallway stuns. I don't usually do this, I say. I don't go into strange men's houses. Never. He leaves me and shoots barefoot into the kitchen to go to the fridge. Okay, he'll leave the door open if I like, he shouts back. I know I should be more charitable, more trusting, but I can't take chances. 'Thanks,' I say, expecting him to be annoyed with me.

He returns with that smile and slaps a pink glass filled with clinking ice into my hand. 'It's okay,' he says, intentionally brushing my arm with his as he passes. 'I don't blame you. I'm no gentleman.'

We go into a white room with a white blind pulled half-way down over French windows. I sit on a white leather sofa with chrome legs. The carpet is off-white and spotless. In front of me is a low, round glass table with a collection of paperweights in the center. One is a dandelion clock caught in round Perspex, arrested before it blows away. There are shelves along the entire length of one wall holding books, junk, a TV and video. Behind me, level with my head on the wall are pictures. Disturbing pictures. I don't like to stare too obviously but they appear to be pen-and-ink cameos of women being sadistically treated by men.

He asks my name.

'Rosy, with a 'y',' I say.

30

'Sad Rose.' He laughs softly; it's more of a sigh than a laugh.

'Why do you say I am sad?' I say, smiling tightly. I refuse to sit back in the squashiness of the sofa and stay bolt upright on the edge instead. The pink drink is Campari and soda, which has never been one of my likes. I gulp it down, wondering if he's put something in it.

'I saw you at the bus stop. So sad. You were crying. One of the most beautiful sad women I've seen.' He cocks his head on one side and considers me for a moment. 'No,' he corrects himself, 'the saddest.'

'Oh, really,' I protest.

He's sitting on the floor about four feet away from me, legs crossed like a Manx symbol, bits of dirt on the soles of his feet. His shaved skin is so smooth I'd like to reach out and touch it. He looks up, deep in thought. Then, he lowers his head and looks at me from those shadowed eyes and I feel an automatic response in parts of my body I'd like to think were hibernating. He's a fast mover. Too fast. Be careful I don't slip up.

'Listen,' he says, and recites poetry to me:

O Rose, thou art sick!
The invisible worm
That flies in the night
In the howling storm,

Has found out thy bed
Of crimson joy
And his dark secret love
Does thy life destroy.

31

'Appropriate?' he says. 'I think so.'

I try to ignore the reference and ask who is the poet. It's William Blake. Of course. Are you a lecturer, too, I ask? No, he's not. He's a solicitor and has taken the day off because the weather is nice. On the first day he saw me, his decree absolute arrived. A silence falls between us. I never felt like this with Zack as I do now—under pressure. Or threat, perhaps. I feel what I do from now on is preordained. The hollow thought strikes me: all resistance is merely a sin of pride, an act. Why can't I admit to myself his looks alone turn me on?

'I want to talk to a woman,' he is saying quietly, 'without taking her to bed, but I want to be intimate. Do you know what I mean? Intimate.' The last word rolls off his tongue and he nods his head at me. What does he mean? Am I the lucky charm he fancied the day his divorce came through? Interrupting my thoughts he asks me questions about my life. Cautiously, I tell him the bits I don't mind parting with, but I feel he knows what's between the lines. I tell him that Zack and I are good friends and watch his mouth twitch, aware of my lie. I tell him about my green house and wild garden, that there are no children. I tell him about Carol, and that I'm thirty.

'It's over,' I say and only then do I realize fully it is. Zack and I were finished in my head, before now, but not in my emotions. This man has managed to prize apart my armor and sink a knife into my weak spot so it cries out in pain. I choke back the tears and the drink jerks out of the glass. Pink

32

Campari spills onto the white carpet. I jump up immediately, spilling more, and apologize as though I've cut off his arm or leg by mistake and not merely spilt liquor on his carpet. I make for the kitchen to find a cloth. Before I reach the doorway he's up and has me by the arm. 'Leave it,' he says. I can't do that. It's a woman's instinct to try and rub out all the stains in the world, isn't it? For a moment it gets ridiculous—both of us jammed in the doorway, me trying to rush for a cloth, him pulling me back in the room. I can hear myself apologizing, all wound up.

Somehow he stops me and I calm down. 'That was very undignified,' he says matter-of-factly. He may not be angry—I wish he was—but I still feel foolish and clumsy. I look at the stain, hideously obvious. I want to lick it up. '. . . And because of it I'm going to spank you,' he says in the same even tone of voice, as if I've been looking forward to a spanking all my life. And he does.

Sunflowers always turn their massive heads to face the sun. It's called heliotropism. The second his arm goes around my waist, I find I have moved to where he wants me to be as though I've been drawn by the pull of some unseen force. I move there naturally until his hand is poised above the blue seat of my jeans. Then I feel the first male invasion of my body in six months. It's a shock. A delicious shock.

After several slaps he lets me go and guides me gently back to the sofa, while he sits on the floor in front of me. I sink into the white leather softness and cry. He lets me cry for a while then speaks.

'I didn't hurt you.'

I shake my head. No, it isn't that kind of pain.

He sighs, touches my leg with his bare foot. 'I know how it is to wall yourself up.' He slides across the floor on his backside to reach up and get a box of tissues from the bookshelf. 'I just took down a few bricks.'

When I've recovered, I ask him if he's crazy. He smiles, shakes his head, turns the questions once more on me. Why do I think a stain on a carpet is more important than human suffering? Why do I look down self-consciously as though I was ashamed of my face? Yes, he's noticed my fingers covering my cheeks, mouth, always there checking, always fluttering. Yes, he can see I'm not wearing any makeup. But ordinarily I do, don't I? Yes, he thought so. Tugging at my fringe, tut, tut, trying to pull a shutter over my eyes. I mustn't wear anything on my face. No. My skin is perfect. My lips are soft, hesitant. My eyes hold a sparkle. I must promise not to paint my face any more, unless he tells me to.

He speaks slow, soft, and I am totally unsure how to react. He tells me I have little confidence, I am paralyzed with hurt. I have stopped growing. I am frightened to find out who I really am. It will change, he says, but I must open myself to new experiences. I must move on.

He stops and it is like the end of a speech on a subject he has studied for years. I watch him stretch out now and push his bare toes through the pile on the carpet. I am in a state of shock. 'Your breakup. . . .' I begin, but he cuts me off. Tells me he does not wish to talk about it, but adds with a grim smile, he thinks he has recovered from the hurt. I want to probe. He's so together and I'm just beginning to fall apart after it's all over. How does he cope?

'I ought to go,' I say. I want to run from this man and think about everything that has happened in the dim privacy of my house. I want to make sense of it all.

He goes out of the room, leaving me sitting on the sofa. When he returns he brings a small sandwich on a plate. 'It's cheese,' he says. He goes to hand me the plate, but before it reaches me, he pulls it back and puts it on the glass table next to the paperweights. He goes out of the room again and comes back with an old silver knife. Picking up the two triangles of bread he begins to pare away the crusts in quick, neat movements. Then he cuts the sandwich in half, then in quarters, and lays the plate on my lap. He eats the crusts. One of his legs is stretched out towards me as he sits on the floor. The heel is resting in the wet patch of Campari, spreading it further. 'You're very sweet,' he says, talking while he is eating. 'I like talking to you.'

I tell him, trying to be impertinent, plucky, that I'm not in such a bad way as he thinks. I've never been smacked before by a man. Never. He eyes me with a curious smile. 'Spanked,' he corrects me. 'The word is spanked.' I argue that children

35

get spanked, not grown women. 'So what,' he says, 'you are little, aren't you?'

I don't want to leave with these words in the air. It would look obvious. He'd know he'd hit a nerve, know I was embarrassed, offended, know it was that last remark which made me go. I look at my watch instead. He says, stay an hour and he'll cook lunch. Fresh linguini, how's that?

I'm surprised, but he has his own garden. He pulls up the blind and opens the French windows wide. Outside is a small patio with a brick-built barbeque and brick seating. Glossy-leaved camellias grow in deliberate gaps between the patio stones, and late summer flowers burst from every crack. There's no lawn but a mass of large plants growing in gravel. A path leads to a dense screen of bamboo. I'm curious to see what lies beyond. Halfway down the path I look back and understand why the garden is filled with tall plants. The maisonettes above have roof gardens which overlook his. The upstairs neighbor has a row of big terracotta pots with little box trees in them, lined up along the front of the balcony, equidistant from each other. 'Who's your neighbor?' I ask. He's behind me with a tray of drinks. Two full glasses of soda with ice and ditto Campari. I feel I want to tell him I'd prefer something else—gin, for instance. I'd also prefer to be asked what I'd like. He shrugs and looks up. 'A woman,' he says simply. 'Do the box trees say anything?' I comment, trying to sound clever. He considers their tall, clipped upright form for a minute, frowns, then

36

laughs to himself. 'She might be short of a prick,' he says.

Behind the bamboo the garden tries to be Oriental. The gravel has been raked into patterns. There are large white stones in careful groups beside a pond. Stiff yucca and a fatsia bow into the area from the boundary fence, which is high and private. There is a row of canes leading away from the pool. They are very close together, their tops cut at different lengths forming a gentle curve. More canes, uncut this time, break away from the first row at right-angles. A thin rattan roof sits on the top, fixed to supporting poles. Half in the shade is a sun bed with a newspaper scattered underneath, the pages muddled up. 'Sit down,' he says. I do so, but gingerly. One of these beds collapsed on me once at Zack's mother's when I lay down on it.

He sits down a little way from me on a narrow path surrounding the pool. He tugs at his jeans, pulling them up to his knees. His legs are quite hairy. With a sigh he sinks each foot into the water.

'There were fish,' he laughs suddenly, 'I guess I've killed them off.'

The sun is surprisingly hot. I'm glad I'm wearing my hair in a plait. Coyly I wonder how he'd like it if I wore my hair down. He hasn't seen me like that.

I am sweating in my jeans. He tells me the next time I come I must bring a swimsuit. No, not a swimsuit—a bikini. I'd look delicious in one of those. He sits back, leaning on his arms for support. For a while we don't talk. When he calls the silence, I keep it.

I wonder to myself what he is going to do with me after the linguini, and whether I'm prepared to go along with it. When he coughs I start to bluster. I'm a nice English girl, I say, half-humourously, half in earnest. I don't know a thing about you. I've never done this sort of thing before.

He opens his eyes straight into the sun and snorts. I know, he says, you don't want me to think you're a hungry little divorcée.

'I think you've played the good girl for too long.'

He may be right. I don't seem to know who I am these days. I tell him I feel different somehow since my divorce. 'Of course you do,' he says in the same matter-of-fact tone, with the same disarming pause before he speaks. I lower my eyes and ask in a disillusioned whisper how much longer before he says he wants to bed me. He winces but the smile returns. He wags a finger at me.

'Rosy, you offend me,' he says. 'You're a naughty girl. Watch out I don't spank you again.'

I fiddle with the ice in my glass. Ice in the shape of Christmas trees. He says we'll eat about three. We sit in the sun for an hour. I pretend to have fallen asleep. Then he says he wants to massage me before he cooks the linguini. This time I say I'm going and my lips pucker. I get up off the sun bed and he stands up in the pool. I've got him wrong, he says. He just wants to make me feel good. I need to relax. Look how my shoulders have risen. They're practically up to my chin. Really, he says, I should be more trusting. But—and he shrugs—I can go if I like, only he'd be much happier if I stayed.

When I drink something I'm not too fond of, I have this peculiar trait that I have to finish every drop. I always try to conquer my dislikes. It's my nature. I didn't like Zack at first. I thought he was pompous, but I gradually came round. Now, I see this old habit bringing me nothing but trouble again. Campari must be stronger than I think. When I say yes to his offer, I say it with the breath of Campari and green Christmas trees. I don't know why I don't kick myself immediately.

He jumps out of the pond ripping up pondweed with his feet and stands there with it curling round his toes. 'Great,' he says and his thumbs dig through the belt loops on his jeans.

I follow him into the house feeling apprehensive and excited. Since February I haven't put a foot out of line.

Impulsively he takes my hand and leads me to a door in the hall. He finds it hard to open, as if there's a weight on the other side, and he gives it a little shove with his shoulder.

It's a small room, a white box. White walls, carpet, blind, swivel chair—he really gets excited about white, I think—with a pile of record sleeves on the seat. The room is quite warm. On a low glass table, similar to the one in the back room, except this one is rectangular, is a record deck and a mass of hi-fi paraphernalia. There are speakers fitted to the wall—two, three, maybe more, I can't tell because they don't look conventional like mine. No pictures.

On the carpet there are records, hundreds of them, in a long line against the wall. He tells me the room is specially soundproofed—ceiling, walls, door (that's why it's hard to open) and triple glazed. He likes music. He likes to make a noise when he wants to. I ask about the woman upstairs. She can't hear a thing, he says. In here, no one could hear you scream.

I put my hands on the wall, except it doesn't feel like a wall. I shiver. A padded cell. A torture chamber. I stand there and watch while he pulls down the blind and shoves the chair into a corner. He leaves me and returns with an armful of white towels. There are small objects sandwiched between them. Oil, talc, a small chinese bowl.

'Did you shower before you came out?' he asks. I color. 'I don't mean that you smell,' he says, smiling, 'although it might be nice if you did. Everyone has their own bouquet.'

I look away from the glint in his eyes. I want to go—now. He thrusts a large towel at me and tells me to strip off while he gets a heater. I rush out of my clothes and wrap a towel tightly around me, over my bra and pants. I'm keeping them on.

He comes back humming and switches on a small fan heater. A smell which reminds me of new-mown hay circulates in the air. It's vetivert oil. He folds the remaining towels and lays them down neatly on the carpet to make a plinth. He lights a candle and puts it in a small porcelain holder. Lie down and make yourself comfortable, he says. I kneel awkwardly on my towel and stretch out.

The towels on the floor are soft, warm, and my body sinks into them. Relax, he says. Don't be uptight. No one will hear you scream.

I laugh into the towel nervously. I lie still, and wait for him to peel the towel away and lay his hands on my body. The hands of a man I don't know at all. I must be crazy or in a real state of shock, or I'd never allow this to happen. I hear him behind me, moving about, like a conductor preparing to conduct.

'I hope you like music,' he says, 'I'm sure you do. I'm going to put something on to help you relax.'

I'm surprised at his choice, but I recognize the music instantly: 'A Love Supreme' by John Coltrane. Zack had a copy loaned to him by a friend at college. It lay around for ages and he never played it, at least not while I was there. I never told him, but I listened to it a lot. Zack may be left-wing, but he still thinks jazz is dirty.

'Aha, I see you know it,' he says, surprise, then pleasure in his voice. He must be observing every small, intimate reaction of mine to make such a comment without my telling him.

The towel slips from my body. I can feel his eyes staring. Three things happen at once. He shouts a 'No!' of disbelief, slaps the top of my thighs hard and gets to his feet. What am I doing dressed? Don't I trust him? What's the matter with me? I listen for the anger in his voice but again, it's oddly absent. Then he sighs and sinks to his

41

knees beside me. I can keep the towel on if I'm so shy, he says, but he's not going to step further until I take off the rest of my clothes.

As it turns out, he helps me off with my bra and slides the panties down over my legs while I lie on my stomach. He starts the record.

The bass figure feels as though it's in the floor beneath me, throbbing up through my hips and thighs. I'd hardly call it an hypnotic piece, but it certainly demands concentration, so for a while I forget myself. That's right, he says, I have to listen. It's a very disciplined composition, like an Indian Raga, limited notes and all that stuff. Nevertheless, I say quietly, it's an odd choice for a massage.

He throws the towel loosely back over my body and starts on my left calf as he kneels by my feet. 'I won't say,' he whispers, 'your body could turn on a block of stone, or you'll jump up and spoil everything.'

The music is soft and it draws me into the presence of the Great Man, Coltrane, so I begin to lose my self-consciousness. 'Like it harder?' he asks. Yes, please. As hard as you like. Hurt me with your fingers and thumbs and make up for all the starvation I've had since February. We're listening to 'Resolution' now and he turns it down as Trane starts honking. But all throughout he still keeps one hand on my skin.

I can't fight these hands. They're ringing out every shred of resistance from my muscles. It now seems absurd to have been so churlish about undressing. He wants to make me feel good. Why can't I accept it? The truth is, I don't think you get something for nothing in life. And if a person inexplicably gives to me, I feel awkward, obligated. That it's wrong to take without reciprocating. But at the moment I don't care what he does as long as he doesn't take his hands away.

There's almost a religious intensity in the way he manipulates my flesh. He slides his hands up my back from my sacrum, his thumbs on either side of my spine. I realize he's squatting on my thighs, leaning forward on his knees. After ten minutes of this I am delirious with pleasure.

He's sweating now, I can smell it, and pounding my buttocks with his fists, nice and hard. His breathing is slow and controlled. Then, his hands suddenly fly away. I feel naked. I shiver for them to touch me again and I edge on my stomach to where I think he's moved. I look round, and see a face that's too dark, too quiet.

This is the moment to go. Now, come on. Grab your clothes, dignity and run. You know what he expects. What he's going to do. I try to get to my feet, but something like thick leather, a belt maybe, or wider, lands across my buttocks, flattening me to the ground.

'No!' he says. 'I haven't finished.'

My bottom smarts more with surprise than pain. I swallow and press myself into the towel. What now? What next?

I turn and look at him in the silence. He feels not sees my nakedness, not aware of it until here, now. The black curls hang damply on his forehead and his chin and neck shine with sweat. There is a wet stain spreading over the front of his tee shirt.

'I'm going to turn you over,' he says, to the apprehension in my eyes, 'but just before I do. . . .'

He smiles and smacks me hard. Ow! I say. What are you doing? He laughs and his voice purrs. The technique is known as percussion, don't I know? It stimulates the muscles. He will demonstrate. First we have clapping, as it's known . . . he hollows his palms and brings them down in rapid succession on the top of my thighs. Then, if he turns his hands on edge, like this . . . and this . . . He's kneeling now, aiming sharp slaps on my bottom. They don't hurt to any degree, but I feel very embarrassed. Slap-spanks. Suddenly I feel hot. The room is a cell. I can't escape from this man and his strange, frightening compulsion.

Now, his free hand is in the small of my back, steadying himself, keeping me there. 'Nice?' he says, through his teeth, as his fingers run away after the slaps, lower down. . . .

My legs begin to open like a book and his fingers open the pages. The record is stuck on the last groove. Tick tick, tick tick. Apart from the sound the room is quiet. The sound of his hand on my bare skin makes the silence in between almost solid.

He stops and rolls me over. This is it, I think. He's going to fuck me. Technically rape, although he'll say well, I *was* naked at the time. I wait for the sound of a rasping zip, but it doesn't come. Instead he kneels at my feet and lifts them until one ankle rests on each shoulder. He moves in closer and my legs are pushed further over until his head is between my thighs and his mouth inches from my sex. I squeeze my thighs involuntarily against his curls.

His tongue is hot and it makes me rise against the pressure of his hands holding down my thighs. He cups my buttocks and insinuates his tongue still further. I can feel my head in a kind of sick spin, as he licks and sucks me into his mouth. It's obscene. But it's ecstasy. I look at the dark curls between my thighs and I push out my hand to touch them. For a second he stops and looks at me. In that moment, his eyes run up the flushed length of my body. He slaps me again. And then his teeth close around me and shudder together on my clitoris. He bites gently, then harder, each time pausing to let his tongue flick over and around, making me tighten my thighs and try to stretch both legs. I am lost now, using him and I don't care about the consequences. He stops, starts, stops until I am on the edge of coming. I begin to plead with him.

'What?' he says.

'I want . . . ooh! . . . .'

'Say it! Ask me! Louder!'

'Please. . . .'

'Please what?'

'Let me come!'

'. . . Say it louder. Come on! Scream! Let it out!'

Please. Ple-ase!

I do as he says. I scream. He puts words into my mouth and I repeat them.

'Say it!—I want to come with your tongue in my cunt.'

LOUDER.

'Yes. Yes. I want to . . . come with. . . .'

'Your tongue up my cunt.'

And then his whole mouth takes me in like a glove and I burst out of all the seams. The first wave rolls over, a tidal wave rushing for my womb. Then his fingers push, moving, moving, his nails dig into my buttock and the orgasms break away uncontrolled.

When later I dress, I find my jeans hurt me as I pull them over my hips.

We eat linguini and he drops some on the white carpet where he grinds it into the pile with his heel.

'You owe me,' he says darkly. 'Don't forget that, if you're thinking about not coming back.'

I ask him what he means.

His face grows serious and the black eyes become frightening, intense.

'What do you think I did after you'd orgasmed yourself to death, eh?'

I blush deeply. Well, he says, he kept his word. I had a good time didn't I? Of course, he wanted to fuck me, what normal man wouldn't? Instead, he went to the bathroom, masturbated. Oh, he could have taken me, raped me. Yes, he could have done that. No other man doubtless would make such a sacrifice.

46

So there we are. Quite simply, he serviced me. A service requires payment. He doesn't want me to forget that.

Payment. What kind of payment does he mean?

4.

Saturday, two days before the start of the autumn term at college. I feel reluctant to go back. I'm uneasy about seeing Zack again, having to talk to him about lessons and timetables, truculent students and sets of books, the one-time intimacy of our lives taboo.

I wake up and find my watch has stopped at 5:17. It's never done that since I was given it nine years ago for my 21st. I shake it hard and bang it on my palm but the hands stay put. Maybe it's an omen, the old life ending, but what next?

Drawing back the curtains I find it's raining. So much for the hot weather. I open the window to relieve the stuffiness. I want to leave it open at night but I can't. At this time of year the spiders come indoors and stare at me from the tops of walls. There's only me now to cope with them. I lean out of the window for a while, feeling the

48

city rain on my skin. I turn my face up and some falls on my lips. It doesn't taste like rain but salty-sour vinegar.

After two slices of toast and some tea I sort out some of my clothes and lay them on the bed, trying to arrange them in groups which match. Some things I find embarrass me and I put these sixties relics into a carrier bag for the Children's Society shop. I haven't given much thought about what to wear since February.

This weekend there's a carnival in the park. There's always something going on during late summer weekends. Customized Audi's drive slowly round like a motorcade, bringing sound systems to set up, and the scent of grass drifts through the trees. Zack and I went to the London carnival in Notting Hill some years ago, before it got so much attention from the media and police. I think the one we have here is better.

At 11 a.m. the music starts. The park is a five minute walk from my house and I can hear the bass speakers even with the windows closed. The sound seems to permeate the crust of the earth, spreading out for some distance from its source like the shock-waves from an earthquake. A sound-quake.

The day seems as grey to me as the weather. I decide to walk over and see what is going on. I put on my jeans and a thin waterproof and take an umbrella. Taking a shortcut through the pub car-park, I realize it's the first time I've been to any event on my own, and the first time to the park for three years. Zack was never very keen.

I cross the road and go in at one of the park entrances and stop. I could phone Holly or Midge. Going to a carnival on a wet day, alone, seems masochistic. But I decide not to turn back. I guess I need to be on my own.

Since Wednesday afternoon I've done some futile preparation for college, but spent most of the time thinking about him. Of course I can't see him again. I could never look him in the eye. Zack never spanked me. And I knew this man for all of three hours, and allowed him to bring me to orgasm the way he did. I feel my face burn at the memory. No one has the right to take me over like that. I'm not ready. But for the past three nights I've imagined his dark hair between my thighs, I've looked down over my naked body in bed and seen him there. It's been only too easy to make use of it, though. And afterwards, I've felt so ashamed.

I walk past the walled graveyard with saplings growing out of graves, and the ranks of Victorian headstones, down to the lake. Rain plays on the grey surface and the four large willows on the edge are still. As I continue up through the poplar avenue the noise gets louder. Forty or fifty sound-systems are in competition. The bass lines are like outbreaks of thunder and the chip-chip, pink-pink of scratchy reggae, the throbbing generators and shrill whistles are all mixed up. I walk over the railway bridge between two skips full of stinking rubbish, and there it is.

In a rough square between the trees, marquees and vans occupy an area about the size of three football pitches. Many shelter under the trees which are looped with cables and hung with home-made signs and scribbled tariff boards, the prices running in the rain. The smell of barbequed sweet-corn and meat patties hangs in the air. Large black ladies fry heaps of onions and sausages over splut-tering gas stoves, suddenly bursting into great trembling laughs. I go in closer.

The noise is a solid undercurrent of heavy bass with sudden surges of bass-beat coming out on top. People are talking to one another by guess-work. I'm glad I wore boots. The grass is hidden beneath a skin of liquid mud that slides about mak-ing patterns as I walk. It takes me a few minutes to work out what is going on, and where. There never appears to be any organization at all, yet everything moves in the same direction. It's the spontaneity of people that makes the carnival happen.

I decide to circuit the stalls and vans on the outside and spiral my way in towards the middle. The center of the mud is monopolized by rival sound systems. They face all directions, stacked like staggered pyramids nine feet high, covered with polythene sheeting that lifts and shudders with sound. Cables run back to vans, to P.A.'s and consoles, banks of switches and black guys with mikes moving about inside them. They engi-neer the music, can't let it alone. They scratch, rap, buzz, stop, play-back and computerize the sound. Each track sounds similar to its predeces-sor. I look at the people moving from one foot to the other in front of the speakers, wooed by rap-chat. They dance to one posse for a while, then amble on.

The bass-feed of a large speaker-stack growls into life near me and the sound hits me in the chest and stomach, making me vibrate with it in time. I close my eyes for a second and let it feel its way through me.

Everyone is drinking. There's no carnival without it, and so I make my way across the mud, through the wandering groups of teenage boys to one of the many trestle tables under the shelter of the trees. I ask the price of Red Stripe, which is what everyone drinks here. The black guy eyes me up and down. You want the price, he says? I nod emphatically. He licks his lips, making up his mind. I look at him and grin. He grins. 'For you, a pound,' he says.

I am about to take the can when from behind, someone intercepts it. I turn and see black eyes glinting at me and a smile of mock-reproof. It's *him*. He puts a hand on my hips and lifts my chin.

'Hello,' he says.

I can't meet his stare and look down. I notice he's wearing mud-soaked plimsolls.

'Hi.'

He pulls me out from under the trees and rips off the ring-pull to my can of beer. He puts it to his lips and drinks.

'You shouldn't,' he says, 'at this time of day. It'll ruin your complexion.'

'Well thank you,' I say, and turn away so he won't see the embarrassed smile that hides beneath my indignation. Laughing, he spins me around in

52

the mud and kisses me hard on the mouth. I taste
my beer on his lips.

'What are you doing?' he shouts. Normal conversation is impossible above the throbbing noise.
'Are you on your own?' I nod. If I say anything
he'll have to move in close to hear me.

He takes my hand and marches me back to
where I bought my beer and the same guy charges
him £1.30 for a Red Stripe. He winces, searches
through his wet pockets for the cash.

'I noticed you flirting with this man,' he says
in my ear, 'I shan't forget that.' His fingers dig
briefly into the outside of my thigh and pinch me
hard. Then he gives me back my beer, three-
quarters full.

'I've been thinking about you,' he says.

He's crazy. His clothes are soaking. No waterproof, only jeans and a thick, ribbed sweater. No
socks, just sodden tennis shoes. Do you have a
thing about getting wet, I ask? For answer he puts
his can and mine into the mud and pushes me
against the trunk of a tree, behind a small tent.
Dark wet curls come down over his forehead
nearly to the eyes. I notice stubble on his cheeks.
The corners of his mouth twitch as he moves in.
Pushing his body against mine so we are joined
from the waist down to our knees, he flicks the
curls suddenly, sending rain drops over my face.
The wet smell of him, the body-contact, the boy-
ish playfulness makes me feel faint.

'Remember?' he says, his wet face against my
ear.

53

I remember.

People walk past and stare at me. My eyes are wide and flickering, as if it is only my body that has to undergo this embarrassing indignity, and my mind is somewhere else. He kisses me as if my mouth is a large juicy peach he is trying to eat. His hands grope at the inside of my thighs. What am I supposed to do? Let him make such a public display of lust? No! Please! I say. 'Don't.' He pulls back and our wet legs part. Before the smile returns a cold look crosses his face. I feel I've said something I'm going to pay for later on.

In a while I get used to him bending close every time we talk. I finish my beer, throw the can on the ground and stamp on it like everyone else does. He wags a finger at me and sends me to buy another so he can watch me flirt again with the guy selling them.

During a heavy squall we shelter underneath a hat stall. There's not one square inch of space on the roof, sides and table in this tiny selling space. He eyes the hats as the rain sheets down and he picks a black homburg with a red fabric band around the crown, pulling it down over his eyes. A hat for ten pounds. I laugh, imagining him wearing it with his expensive suit. Impulsively he digs into his pocket. I am aware of the top half of his face in shadow. Only his thin nose and wide mouth are visible. The mouth, by itself, is cruel. There is something erotic about the way he wears this hat, and my guts shiver. Never before have I been led astray by a man's looks.

The stall sells hats for men, not women. I see

what I think is a pile of fluffy berets and am surprised when a male arm reaches over my shoulder and tries one on. It's a kind of angora beret with a peak. That's the basic shape of all the others, hanging from the roof like bats, and they're so round and wide I'd be lost in them.

He sees me looking and selects a cap made from many pieces of brown and cream leather stitched together, throwing it on my head. I look in the mirror, giggle and it wobbles, falls. He catches it before it lands in the mud.

After a while we walk out into the rain. He marches me up to a stacked speaker tower and guides my body back against the plastic-covered speakers. The vibrations go through my chest, jump on my diaphragm and make the skin on the tops of my legs and arms shiver. Stay there, he mouths silently and takes my umbrella, balances it upright on his hand and holds it out to me. It dances like a gyroscope. I laugh and the sound becomes a vibration. He drops the umbrella in the mud and puts his hand against my crotch. 'Do you feel it here?' he asks.

The sky is low and grey and his arm is tight around me. Where he goes, I go too. For a minute I am shocked by the thought that it feels as though we have always been together. I must be careful. He has a way about him that makes me do what he wants.

A lorry drives slowly down one of the park roads to the far football pitch. On the trailer is a young steel band. They wear grey track suits with pink logos on their chests, and the same word appears on every piece of tin: 'MAXIES.' The lorry lurches over a ramp and the players, along with their sawn-off drums high on shiny stands, slide a foot or so, but no one loses balance. Behind me, he is licking the raindrops from my neck.

We move with others in a meandering crowd to the park entrance. More lorries, more floats come in off the main street. The barriers on either side of the entrance are ignored. People push in front of them. Large ladies in pink with soggy hats and jiggling torsos stand on the edge of the road. Their stomachs sway and wobble to the music coming from the floats. A black man comes towards us out of a procession of dancers dressed in long red and gold costumes. He has a whistle in his mouth, a small stick in one hand and a large shaker of Imperial Leather talc in the other. Blowing the whistle as he breathes, he weaves in and out of the gold, red and ribboned feet, and comes to the crowd, puffing talc in our faces. One of the large pink ladies gets a puff and she joins him in the middle of the road for a minute. They roll their hips around each other with an innocent intimacy I find faintly shocking. Then she turns, curtseys to him back-to-front and he gives her large bottom a crack with his stick as the procession moves on. She comes back to us, staggering, dragging her feet, laughing tears.

'How would you like me to do that to you?' he says in my ear, 'in front of all these people? Would you blush? I bet you would.' His hands are tight around my waist, squeezing me, and his

56

breath is warm on my wet cheek. Our thighs are glued, making heat.

'I think you are obsessed,' I say.

'Absolutely.'

'Are you? . . . .'

'Looks like it.'

I sigh. It's hard to keep control of my thoughts. As we watch the rest of the procession he bends his head every so often—almost absently—and flicks aside my plait to make little staccato spots on my neck with his tongue. I squirm but his grip around my waist always tightens. 'What are you thinking?' I say.

'What you taste of,' he replies. 'I was just trying to put a name to it.'

Three policemen opposite stare at us and I feel myself going red. There aren't many white faces among the crowd, so we stand out. I watch as they lean into one another, grinning, pointing fingers in our direction. 'Do they know you?' I say. 'They're laughing at us.'

He stops attending to my neck and looks at the men. 'One was in Court last week,' he says, and sardonically doffs his hat. My ear is wet all over now by his repeated assaults on it.

The floats come on and on in the rain. More steel bands, more clashing music. People dance on the open-sided lorries as they pass. A group with purple and white feathered costumes jump along the road, their massive feather fans whirring above their heads. Ordinary men and women follow them, drinking, kissing, and blowing their

57

whistles. When the last lorry has edged through the crowd we walk back after it, overtaking the floats as they make their way to the judging area. My body moves with each different rhythm as we pass.

He makes me dance very close to him. We rub our bodies together, up and down. He lifts my arms and bends me back, our feet moving one and two, one and two, and leans over me, pressing his thighs tight against mine. Other couples are doing it too. We're whites aping the blacks and they cheer us on.

A young black jumps down from a calypso trailer and breaks into our dance. 'Hey man, how you doin' he says, throwing his arms around him, me, and shaking our hands. He passes us a joint and it's an insult to refuse. I feel a rush of heat to my head, the world seems more vivid and I fall against him, laughing.

'I got the guy off and he never lets me forget it,' he says as the young man leaps back onto the trailer again.

He gets excited at the discovery of some live music being played in a trailer further down. He wants me to hear, to move, to *feel*. It's a funk band. A Rasta drummer, white guitarist and a half-caste youth on a bass with a sawn-off neck. Two black guys front the band.

He pulls me closer until we stand mid-way between the speakers. There is a rawness, an energy about the music. They do James Brown's 'Sex Machine' and the crowd starts moving behind us. Next to me a heavy black in a leather jerkin rolls himself a neat roach from the cigarette-paper packet, snapping his fingers loudly at the same time.

'The band is from London,' he says, 'Too good for round here.' I catch the fire in his eyes, almost like lust, as we get all roused up by the sound.

I've always been a good mover but I lost the unselfconsciousness for dancing when I was with Zack. Now, the beer and the company and the noise begin to peel away my inhibitions. Slowly, in time to the music, I undo my plait, take off my waterproof and jumper and lay them on the ground. He watches me, the smile on his face alight, and puts a hand over his eyes in a mock gesture of shock. He thinks maybe I'm going to strip. Instead I show him what I can do with my body even though I'm wearing boots and jeans.

We stay all afternoon listening to the bands. He buys hamburgers with chilli relish, so hot I can barely eat them, and grilled salt fish. We chew our way through foot-long pieces of sugar cane, peeling it with our teeth and chewing the wood until all the sweetness has gone before spitting out the fibers. He buys me a silver metal whistle on a length of tape.

We join the crowd in front of the heaviest system in the park. Here, everyone likes to get close in to the magic plexus of the sound. Suddenly there's pushing, hustling towards the unseen center like a rugby scum and there's barely room to breath among all the bodies. It happens several times and I get separated from him and push against the tide to get back. He puts his arms over my shoulders and links his fingers behind my neck, winding my loose hair around them. We don't try and talk but just move and the bass—which is what everyone comes to experience—becomes anaesthetic.

Because of the low cloud it quickly gets dark. He buys me a little green light which glows when bent in half and hangs it around my neck with the whistle. 'I don't want to lose you,' he says, 'or, for you to get away from me again.' He buys me a huge balloon with something inside it that sounds like maracas when I jerk it on the string. More people recognize him. A middle-aged West Indian man buys us each a white rum in plastic cups. We drink and eat with it pieces of a pale-brown coconut-type fruit.

As the evening wears on he is offered some 'smoke.' He buys £5 worth in a small screw of brown paper, after sniffing it briefly and rubbing some between his fingers. 'Now,' he says, turning to me. 'I need a safe place to put this,' and he stuffs the paper inside my blouse, poking it down until it's wedged inside my bra. His fingers linger on my breasts. 'Remember,' he says, his mouth at my ear. 'You owe me.' His body is as tight as a sandwich to mine.

It is late evening. There seems to be nothing in the world but the carnival and the noise. It becomes an orgy of letting go, losing your identity. People crash into each other as they lumber from foot to foot in front of loudspeakers, drunk on beer, grass and sound. The ground is all cans and empty bottles, cigarette butts glowing in the mud, chips and half-eaten pies sliding out of their paper wrappings. I do not want to leave. I want to stay until the last throbbing note dies away in the air.

At length he says, 'Let's go,' and we walk back across the park. I'm grateful to have him with me. Grateful, but scared. The hubub of noise recedes. We hear our feet scrunch along the stony track between the poplars. The silence of the dormant park seems huge. I still hold the balloon and don't quite know what to do with it. He takes it from me, looses the string, gives it a punch and it bounds away over the grass in the moonlight for a child to find next day.

The moon silvers the poplars which, when I look up, appear to rise and stretch in the sky. At the bottom of the path we slow and he stops to look at the water. It's raining again, but not hard and the moonlight wavers on the surface. He sighs and I realize at that moment who I am, who he is, and that we have spent a day together like long-term lovers.

The black hat is tilted so his eyes are hidden. His profile makes me ache as he kicks stones into the water.

'You weren't going to see me, were you?' he says.

It's a shock to hear his voice as it really is; quiet, smooth, so intense. Perhaps the man who shouted in my ear at the carnival was someone else. I feel myself sinking inside, not knowing what to say. Earlier it seemed we were together in a conspiracy of fun. Now the scales have been tipped abruptly and I've lost my balance. Immedi-

61

ately, so inappropriately, I remember the feel of his tongue between my legs. How did I manage to forget it this afternoon?

'I thought you'd back out,' he says. 'You weren't going to come back, eh?'

I can't answer and I feel like a silly schoolgirl, standing tongue-tied in the rain, waiting for the reckoning which will spoil all that's gone before.

'Why?' His hands pluck the wet denim from his thighs. 'Why? Tell me.'

I take a breath. 'I was ashamed of myself.'

He looks up. I catch the glint of his teeth.

'Ashamed?' he echoes with a snort. 'You've got nothing to be ashamed of.'

'I have,' I say. 'I let myself go, and I've never. . . .'

'What?' He waits for an answer, plucking the wet clothes from his body, feeling their discomfort for the first time.

'Never . . . Before I've always. . . .' I shrug. The words don't come easily.

'Had oral sex? Is that what you're trying to say?'

I might have expected sarcasm in his voice, but there's none, just matter-of-factness. I look up at the face in shadow under the hat.

'What I mean is . . . I've never just *taken*. Lied there. Done nothing else. I feel it's kind of wrong.'

He grins broadly. 'You were embarrassed!'

'Yes.'

'A little humiliated?'

'A little.'

'Anything else?'

'Guilty, I guess.'

He's laughing now, making fun of me. 'You must be unusual. Or . . .' there is a pause into which his laughter dies away, '. . . very masochistic.'

I turn away to look at the lake. 'I just felt powerless, that's all.'

'But you enjoyed it.'

I do not give him an answer.

He reaches out and puts his hands in my hair, fluffing it out with his fingers and pulling at the tangles. His movements are gentle but I sense he is annoyed and that any moment he might suddenly tug hard, to hear me cry out. 'Undo me,' he says.

Only for a second do I consider not doing what he asks. Then my fingers go uncertainly to the top of the zip. It's wet and hard to slide. Taking one hand away from my hair, he frees the zip and takes out his penis, which is half-erect. 'You mustn't feel afraid of me,' he whispers as he closes my hands around it. Immediately, my hands grow wet and warm. I pull them away, shocked, but he slaps them back again, before continuing. My jeans and jacket become wet. I hold my breath, feeling trapped, near to tears. I cannot move my hands. They are frozen as this warm rain runs through them.

He separates my clasped hands and zips his trousers. 'There,' he says smoothly, 'I've recipro-

63

cated. Now you won't feel so ashamed, eh? Satisfied?'

I want to go home, I say.

With a shrug of his shoulders he walks off. I follow him. He is silhouetted in the moonlight. I try to work out that walk, that body—what it all means. I can't. My feelings toward him are not objective any more. I run after him trying not to make my footsteps sound obvious.

'Have I offended you?' I ask.

He stops, looks down at me and smiles. 'Whatever makes you think that?'

Beside the graveyard wall the dark becomes dense, palpable. The only light comes from a street lamp some two hundred yards away on the road. Suddenly I get a panicky feeling he's going to run off because my fear might amuse him. I move closer, touching his arm with mine.

When I was a child I lived in the country where there were no street lamps. The dark there fell like chaos. I never got used to it. In our quiet cottage, every dark room held a horrible secret. Always that fumble for the light switch, the cold hand about to close over my fingers before I made it. In winter the being pressed its nose to the windows. It fed on blackness, hated light and wanted to destroy it. I couldn't be left in the house alone at night. I hated upstairs where sleep, night and dark took over.

'Frightened of the dark?' he says, reading my mind again.

'I used to be.'

He chuckles softly and takes my hand in his. 'D'you think I'd leave you?' he says, 'When I've spent the last few days looking for you?'

We cross the road and go through the empty pub car-park. In a minute he'll know where I live. I don't know how I'll cope with the knowledge he may call on me then, at any time.

'You will have some coffee?' I say carefully as we walk up to my door. No, he says, laughing. He won't. He wants to run home and get out of his wet clothes. I am surprised, put out. Oh, I say, but would you mind waiting just a minute while I go in? I have a terror of burglars.

The house is dark. I'm glad of him standing in the doorway while I turn on all the lights. He looks into the hall, tilting the wet homburg further down over his face. I keep him waiting while I run upstairs and check the bedrooms. I'm being silly. I don't need him to stay while I do this.

'Right,' he says, 'Okay? I'm off.' As I come back downstairs he blows me a kiss, touches his hat and backs away from the door before jogging out of sight up the road.

For some time I stand in the doorway, feeling dismayed before closing the door. I had expected more—a kiss, maybe more than a kiss? Ruffled, I take a shower and sit downstairs in my night-clothes, a short cotton nightdress with two kissing teddy bears on the front and a matching kimono. I can't go to bed. I'd never sleep. Instead I fuss about the house, doing unnecessary jobs. My jeans smell of urine and I gather clothes together to wash them. In the garage I can't see the way to the washing machine at the far end because the bulb has gone. In a sudden funk I throw all the clothes on the floor and shut the adjoining kitchen door which leads into the garage, quick. The old fear comes back.

It's past midnight. I've been watching 'The Postman Always Rings Twice.' The voices in the room comfort me. For some reason I'm convinced I can't go to bed. I'm not sure why. Maybe I'm scared.

A car pulls up outside. It's Mr Singh, the neighbour, coming back from one of his late night drinking clubs. A smooth-sounding engine, whose sound dies away in the silence. In a minute he will have woken the house and be shouting at his wife. I sigh and go into the kitchen to make myself some tea. From where I stand I see a figure outside my glass front door. I swear to myself. I have the neighbour's spare key, though it's pointless trying to let himself quietly into the house if he wakes them all up with his shouting. Yes, he's there now, arm raised, about to ring my bell.

I am on my way to the door with the spare key. I put the chain across, although it's not much use. It wouldn't stop anyone shouldering the door if they wanted to. Mr Singh? I call, but the moment I open the door a crack, I know I've got the wrong man.

It's him. He's wearing a cream sweater and black cords. He smells clean, like he's showered too.

'Let me in,' he says.

I shut the door, take the chain off and open it

66

again. There's a car in my drive—not a Porsche, but almost. Metallic silver glints in the moonlight.

He walks straight in, shuts the door behind him and locks it, pocketing my keys. I back away from him into the kitchen. 'What is it?' I say. He doesn't answer. I move to the cooker and fiddle with the controls. He just leans against the open kitchen door and stares at me in a way that makes me sweat.

'What are you wearing under that?'

I look down at the kimono. It's wrapped tightly around me and the belt is tied in a little bow.

'What do you want?' I say.

He nods at me. Slowly I undo the belt.

'Is this what you want?'

He stares at me for a long time with eyes so intense they are cruel. The hissing of the gas under the kettle makes me aware I'm not dreaming. 'Why are my keys in your pocket?'

No answer.

Leather soles tap quickly across the room towards me. He turns off the gas and before I slip past to run, he has me by the arm, pulling the kimono from my shoulders, deliberately ripping it. We struggle.

'I'm not going to let you do this to me!' I cry, but he is strong. Hauling me to the kitchen table, he pushes me down onto it with my legs hanging over the edge towards him. Futilely I clutch the nightdress in my fist between my thighs, as I try to roll away from his hands. I get one foot against his stomach and push, but he grabs my ankle and pulls me closer to him. Then he leans over me,

67

pinning me to the table with his forearm while his free hand tears at my nightdress. I am dragged forward, my legs forced up until they bend at the knees, when he knocks them open. I hear him struggle with the zip of his trousers. He lifts me, gripping my buttocks and then, the moment, the breaching, as he thrusts deep. I cry out.

He fucks like an animal. Fast, without thought, with much noise. His breath is shallow, desperate, and in it I detect a note of anguish. My insides begin to feel formless. He looks down at me as he thrusts, wondering what I am. When he comes he cries out on one gasping inbreath, sinking down, clutching my body, scoring my hips with his nails. His hands slam down on the table either side of me and he drops his head on my belly. He looks dark, in pain.

I lift myself up, reach out, and stroke his curls.

5.

I don't see him at all the following day. I expect him to call early in the morning—doesn't he want more of what he had last night? I know I do. Or was that it, a quick release for him, and then goodbye? He said nothing to me last night. After it was over he pulled me off the table and set me on my feet and the rawness between my legs throbbed. He lifted his chin and looked at me with an expression I could not work out. A kiss as soft as a breath, a quick smile and he was gone. I ran upstairs to watch him drive away.

By lunchtime disillusionment sets in, and then anger. Like the fast mover he is, he's probably picked up another lucky charm at the bus stop. He's a one-off guy, and he's had his way with me.

It rains heavily all day, but still the carnival carries on. But I don't go back. I might see him.

I might not. He may come to the house when I'm out. I'll go, trying to relive yesterday and be disappointed. So, I waste time looking out the window and get more irritable and frustrated as the day goes on. By evening I'm fuming. If he shows now, he'll get a slap in the face! Oh! If only he'd come!

On Monday I go back to work, tired and upset after crying in the night. So I've been used? Well, so what? I mustn't be such an easy victim in the future. It's taught me a lesson. I make a resolution not to think about Saturday. It's not easy. His smile keeps returning. The sound, the feel of him come back. I walk to work instead of taking the bus because the day is grey and I'm grey too.

There are workmen in the park collecting all the litter, sweeping cans into piles. All the grass has gone in places and what is left is battered, used. I find I am thinking about being raped by someone I like. Does that make it rape, I wonder? Technically, it does—he didn't ask my permission. He was my only man since February. For a second I feel almost smug he found me so irresistible. It's going to be hard to find another to take his place.

I always take my mail with me, unopened, to work. This morning I'm grateful for the three letters on the carpet. I don't feel like conversation when I get there. Opening them will give me something to do, a way out.

The college looms up behind ranks of terraced houses. It was once a lodestar of civic borough pride in the Victorian era, when H— was not part of the city, as it is now. The old red bricks have, in certain atmospheric conditions, a matt blueness, a starkness, like the unforgiving walls of a prison. The building sprawls pompously like all the others of its type in the area and is marked out by a clock tower which can be seen for miles.

Apprehensively, I go in through the back entrance. I don't like first days. Two security guards in grey, with walkie-talkies strapped around their waists, are lounging back against a radiator. One has his boot on the small table in front of him. He keeps an oafish eye open for all the women who walk down the corridor. I try to slip quickly past them, but am called back.

It's his job of course to check the identity of everyone who enters the college, but he knows me from last year. He makes a fuss about seeing my card, which I've forgotten, and shifts from boot to boot, winking and signalling to his colleague as I search through my bag. It amuses him to see me flustered. I'm sorry, *Miss,* he says, you know it's policy to check you. I sigh and protest, but this morning I lack confidence and he waves aside my excuses with a broad sweep of his arm. Eventually I tell them to ring the Head of Department on extension 258 and satisfy themselves as to who I am. The Head of Department: Zack. At this they laugh and wave me on. They've had their little game.

I try not to run as I make my way to the staff common room where there is a morning meeting for all part–time staff. I hope I don't meet Zack— yet. Out of breath I reach the end of the long corridor and climb the stairs. I can hear the first

71

tide of students pouring through the main doors at the front.

The meeting has just begun. The principal, a pale, suited man in his late forties is stroking his leather watch strap as a cue for the beginning of his speech. I make my way to one of the empty chairs at the back. There are about ninety of us already in the hall.

Standing down one wall are full-time staff with large labels pinned to their fronts. They eye the part-timers with ill-disguised superiority. They'll make sure we take the unruly classes they don't want.

I study the principal as he introduces himself. He stands super-relaxed, hands in his trouser pockets, swinging his legs a little like he's kicking stones waiting for a bus. Giving out all the body-talk of being approachable and sympathetic, when in the privacy of his office, he has reduced many of his staff to tears. His dark glasses mean you can never read his expression accurately. I've been told he has an eye condition. I think they are a calculated device he picked up in a management training course.

The sycophants at the front, the ones who are new this year, laugh appropriately at his trivial opening anecdote. I look round the room at the new faces. Then I catch sight of someone horribly familiar. Carol—the flibbert. What is *she* doing here?

She drapes herself over the chair with one arm posed so two gold bangles slide down it just past her wrist, giving her a faint aura of seductiveness.

72

She's wearing a russet blouse and skirt to match which goes with her red hair. She's heavily, but expertly, made up. I notice her long legs crossed just above the knees. Legs aimed at the principal's glasses. I think I call her the flibbert because she threatens me and I want to reduce her in my mind to a dumb, flighty female.

I don't think she saw me arrive. Her eyes are fixed sweetly on the principal's mobile mouth. It is possible she didn't recognize me because this morning I am wearing my hair loose, not in its usual plait, as a gesture of defiance. I think about her being here as I pore over the stained glass windows above the little rostrum. She's not a teacher, but a secretary. There are hundreds of people like me who are out of work, and she jumps right in! Even Zack told me she was not as bright as I am, (this was to dull the blow of his leaving) and how much he still respected my mind above all others. Respected! You're supposed to want to hear that kind of thing from a man, but when you do, it hurts. Of course I know how she got the job. She sneaked in through the back door like I did.

One of the perks endemic in this college is getting your partner or spouse a job here too. It's not difficult. When I met Zack I was out of work. He decided, after we married, it would be nice if I worked alongside him. He gave such glowing verbal references to the principal that by the time I was interviewed, I was accepted immediately. When we were still exciting to each other it was great to be near him, to pass in the corridor and maybe steal a kiss or two inside an empty class-room. But after a while I'd notice how he'd look at some of the women. I know it was only just looking, but I used to wish I worked somewhere else then—in an office full of men, for instance. Now, he's got his flibbert here. My replacement.

The administrative officer is speaking now, but I haven't been listening. I've missed all the chat about enrollment; the importance of continuous assessment, reprographics, etc. I know it all anyway. I feel tears of rage and hurt prick my eyes and the lump in my throat is so painful, it's making me choke. As dignified as possible I go out coughing, drowning in my tears. This time she recognizes me. As I look at her she raises her hand and winkles her fingers at me. Every nail is perfect with deep pink varnish, the half-moons clearly visible. I tell myself they've got to be false. They make my nails look monstrous by comparison.

There's nowhere in college to cry. I have to walk down the corridor with my head up. All the students scrutinize me. I have to get away from them all.

I leave the main stream of people and go through a door marked 'Staff.' Up a steep flight of steps I pause at the top and open one of the doors opposite on the landing. Ron Fennell sits with his back to me and as I shut the door, he turns around, throwing his arms wide in greeting.

Ron's due to retire next year. God knows how long he's been teaching here. I can't imagine how he'll cope with nothing to do, when it happens.

'You're lucky,' he says with a nod at the three

empty desks beside his, 'they're all out. We've got the room all to ourselves.'

The room is very small with a window high up the wall, covered on the outside by a metal grille. There's barely enough light to work by. Ron leans against his desk. He knows me. He's known me ever since Zack brought me here. He knows I want to talk.

'Is it about Carol?' he asks perceptively. I nod. He goes to the kettle in the corner and switches it on. His bifocals slip a long way down his nose. I notice his silver hair is so fine, it lifts in a thin cloud as he moves.

I ask how he is, and say I must invite him and his wife Eva for a meal one day soon. He smiles, picks up a large pile of snapshots from his desk and hands them to me. He hasn't been working. He's been poring over his memories. I flick through them quickly, out of politeness. They are mainly photos of Eva. Eva, standing in front of the car with a backdrop of Spanish scenery, Eva, sitting in a cafe finishing paella with dirty plates and spreadeagled forks still on the table, and the white crook of a waiter's elbow rushing out of the picture. He went to see his daughter who married a Spaniard, he says. We caught gastroenteritis on the second day.

By the time he's made coffee I'm feeling a little less hysterical. I sit down and listen while he tells me his domestic troubles, chuckling to himself. He tells me he's got three more holidays booked. A week in the Algarve, ten days in Portugal, and nearer to us, Christmas with his daughter. When he stops talking I ask him about Carol. It's as I

75

thought. She's Zack's new protégé. Ron says kindly he sympathizes with how I must be feeling. Zack is insensitive. But, he says, I mustn't get too upset. I've earnt my place here over the years. He tells me my hair looks nice, in fact I look different somehow—have I perhaps got back on my feet?

I leave after I've had my coffee and go to the third floor staff-room, where all the part-timers in my department have the use of a desk. I arrive out of breath as usual after climbing about four dozen stone steps and collapse gratefully into the chair. The room is noisy. Five full-timers are talking about the new vice principal in cutting tones. The two union reps are bearing down on a middle-aged woman, stuffing papers into her briefcase. I turn my back on them all and open my mail.

One of the letters looks suspiciously tampered with; it's franked and there's a white label on the front typed with my name and address, but still I feel it's been used before. I insert my thumb under the flap and rip it open. (Zack hated the way I opened mail. He had a paper-knife. He also cut the tops from boiled eggs with a knife.)

The large, carefully-folded sheet of paper has a faint scent, like new-mown hay. I unfold it to find a poem, immaculately typed. It reads:

The Constant Lover

Out upon it I have loved
Three whole days together!
And am like to love thee more,
If it hold fair weather.

76

Time shall moult away his wings
Ere he discover
In the whole wide world again
Such a constant lover.

But a pox upon't, no praise
There is due at all to me:
Love with me had made no stay,

Had it been any but she.
Had it been any but she,
And that very, very, face,
There had been a least ere this
A dozen dozen in her place.

I read it once, twice. Underneath the verses is a paragraph written by hand. I hold up the page and scrutinize the writing. Just the way it's crafted, in thin scratchy black ink, makes my pulse begin to beat.

'I had to get up early to make you think this came in the post. Payment—first instalment—received with thanks.

I want you.

V.'

I look round feeling curious eyes reading over my shoulder, but there's no one there. Heat and weakness flush between my thighs and face. Just a few sweet words and I forget my resolutions completely.

The door behind me opens. Zack comes into the room. He has a way of opening doors peculiar to him, easily recognized. He opens them very wide, stands in the doorway and scans the room before stepping over the threshold and letting them swing shut after him.

'Hello, hello,' he breezes, and the quintet in the corner say, 'Hi, Zack.' I hear him hesitate. He knows I am sitting there but he pretends not to recognize me at first, because of my hair. His manner is too-damn-jolly when he's nervous of a situation. He likes to play games, to tease a bit. He comes up to me and walks past, then turns and looks at me with a frown on his face. 'It's you,' he says, trying to sound surprised.

'Hello, Zack.'

'It doesn't look like you. You always wear your hair in a plait.'

The rest of the room goes quiet and he smiles icily at the eavesdroppers. They laugh and talk again, more intimately.

'How are you, Rose?'

I glower at him. It may be childish, but it's how I feel. 'How d'you expect me to feel? I saw Carol at the meeting.'

He pulls up a chair from the next desk and sits on it, front to back, his hands clasped, his chin resting on them. A quick glance and I take in what he's wearing. Loose casual jacket, buff shirt, cotton drill trousers. He's also wearing a very thin tie. I've never seen him wear one to work before. It's always been open-necked shirts and the I'm-one-of-you-brothers image. Now, he's going to the top. He needs a little distance from the others. The equality gets stretched a little.

His voice has dropped to a murmur. He feels guilty. 'Are you okay for bills . . . that sort of thing?'

I feel disgust. I tell him in a clipped voice, I can manage. I notice his fair hair has been permed. I've never liked men who mess with their hair. It's narcissistic.

'Why do you want to hurt me further by bringing Carol here?' I say.

'We can't talk here.'

'We can.'

He bites the quick along the edge of his thumb. It's a habit he's had ever since I've known him. It tells me he's a bit scared of a showdown, of blowing his image of Mr Cool. He says I was okay about his leaving, so why the sudden change? I handled the break-up commendably. I made things easier for him at work.

I find myself thinking of the painting he bought me. Yes, he bought the damn thing so I'd say what a good ex-husband he was to all his colleagues. To show them all we were still friends—he couldn't drop me after seven years. That would be inhumane. Oh, yes, he's done more than he's legally required to do, he's paid all the bills. But it's a good way of making me keep quiet. And it's also kept me suffering.

'Okay,' he says, 'Carol wasn't happy in her job. I thought she might do well here. You shouldn't see her as a threat.'

I laugh bitterly and tears spring to my eyes. Zack can't cope and spins off his chair to make some coffee. The room empties. There's just the two of us.

'Look,' he says. 'I'll take you to Azim's for lunch. We can talk there.'

'What about Carol? Won't she mind? You'll have trouble with her if she finds out.' I choke and tell him I can't switch my feelings off as fast as he'd like. It's cruel to bring me face to face with Carol. I ask him if seven years means nothing.

He gets upset and we can't talk. He looks at the paper on my desk, at the poem, and turns it with his thumb so he can read what it says. I feel uncomfortable.

'Who's this?' he says. It's his turn to be knocked off balance.

'A friend.' I get up and take the poem from him, folding it up.

'What sort of friend?' A frown deepens on his forehead and his mouth pouts a little. 'Well, I'm glad you've met someone else,' he adds, carefully guarding the tone of his voice.

'Someone,' I counter.

'Anyone I know?'

'No. I doubt it.'

'What does he do?'

I smile to myself as I tell him. He gets up. 'I'll know where to come if I need any free legal advice,' he says, and then there is a pause. 'Nice, is he?'

'Different.'

'Not getting yourself into any situations, are you?'

He is annoyed and I'm glad. I hope the last three words on the page are branded in his mind. I think about Carol and her fingernails. I hope she gives him hell with them.

'How long have you known this guy?'

'Not long.'

He stops asking me questions and a thought comes to him. One of his department, Leroy Randall, told Zack he'd seen me at the carnival on Saturday. I was having a good time, he'd said. Zack quizzes me—was I with this solicitor then?

I smile and pick up my bag, making for the door. 'I don't ask you what *you* do,' I say, and go out.

6.

At 4:30, minutes after I get back home, a silver car slides into my drive and parks. It's him. I'm upstairs, looking moodily out of the front bedroom window when I see him drive up. Straight away my legs go weak and I forget my own name. I let him ring the doorbell long and impatiently. I go downstairs. He rings again although he can see me through the glass door. I open it. 'You kept me waiting,' he says.

He's carrying a large flat white box, an over-sized cake box. He pushes his way into the hall before I say anything, and walks into my living room. It's a mess. The Sunday newspapers sit in a muddle. There's a pile of unironed clothes in a chair. The smokey plastic cover on the record deck is dull with dust. All the videos are out of their cases on the rug in front of the fire. Toast crusts still lie on my breakfast plate and there's a recent stain on the carpet where I spilt my tea. He must think I live in squalor like this all the time.

He drops the box onto the sofa and takes off his coat with the velvet collar. He looks terribly sexy in his suit.

I don't know what to say to him. He behaves as though he's forgotten he raped me on Saturday night.

'I see what you mean about the green,' he says, as he looks at the elephants on the wallpaper, and around the room. I think, will my possessions pass? He likes my plants, he says. I must have green fingers. He'd like some in his room with the French windows, but those he buys seem to die on him. Fondly he examines the leaves of a fifteen year old palm, stroking them. Then he returns to the box on the sofa. He unbuttons his jacket, loosens his tie and takes the lid off the box. I am looking at his hands; all the little lines and the knuckles; the way he moves his fingers, the way he has used them on me and I feel heavy between my thighs, as if I am pulled down there. Down, down. I sit down.

'I'm taking you out,' he says. 'I don't expect you've got anything suitable. I bought these for you.'

'Wait a minute,' I say nervously. 'I'm not used to surprises like this.'

I see black chiffon and small packages on top of the delicate folds in tissue paper. The first one is a cream silk suspender belt, edged with lace and with six ruched silk suspenders. I like you to feel the pull on your stockings, he tells me. He

83

will adjust them until they are purposefully very short. Next is a cellophane packet of black silk stockings, seamed. Very expensive. I'm scared to touch them with my less-than-perfect nails. I can't wear these, I say incredulously. I've never worn stockings.

'They're a little fetish of mine,' he laughs. 'You'll wear them for me, Rosy.'

He draws one from the packet and holds it up between finger and thumb, holding it by the toe so it unravels before my eyes. I blush.

'Never worn them?' he says as he runs the silk gently over my left shoulder, across the back of my neck and down the other side. A little tug and the sheerness shivers over my bare neck.

'You'll wear them for me, Rosy,' he murmurs with a hint of menace.

What would Zack say, I think? Stockings to him were a symbol of intellectual female bondage. They were too overt, too sexual. Advertising the woman as a sex object, not a thinking being. Right now I imagine walking in front of him in them, watching the red embarrassment flush over his cheeks, feeling himself going hard despite his politics. But then perhaps he's changed. After all, Carol does paint her nails.

The third package is a pair of silk French knickers, very plain, very expensive, with a lover's knot motif cut into the front of each leg just above the hem. I examine them under his gaze of amusement and lay them beside the stockings on the sofa.

'What do you think?' he says. 'Aren't you a grateful bitch, hmm?'

I see his mind working, picturing what I will look like in these clothes when I put them on. I don't feel easy about accepting such costly presents. I don't want to be bought, to feel obligated. I want freedom, don't I? What might he expect from me if I so readily take all he offers? I've heard about women who find themselves trapped in these situations.

He gives me a shrewd look. 'There's no catch,' he says. 'If I take a woman out she's got to look how I want her to look.'

'No one has spent this kind of money on me before.'

'Really?' His eyebrows rise, mocking me, and a little smile comes and goes.

He lifts the chiffon from the box. It's a dress, a skin-tight one, ruched from breast to mid-thigh, with a handkerchief hem on a slant; no proper straps, just triangular wisps of black which slide over the shoulders. It's like a tube lined with black satiny material and a see–through hem. 'Sexy, eh?' he says, sweeping aside my hair and biting me between neck and shoulder. 'I'll bring in the shoes while you have a shower.'

I'm to shower and call him when I've finished. I'm not to dry myself. I ask him if he sent the poem. He looks at me indulgently. 'Now, who else would send you one?' he says.

I do as I'm told, but God knows why. Perhaps it's because I've never had a man treat me this way. I hope the novelty doesn't wear off. He's making me feel hungry for sex in a way I've never experienced before. It's as if he can see into my psyche and knows what's there, and I don't. It's as if he's telling me I'm the most sexual woman who's ever lived. I'm beginning to believe him, and myself.

I go upstairs and leave him in my living room. I know he's looking at my books, records and all my personal bits and pieces. I know he's building a composite of what I'm like from everything I own. I imagine him flicking through my jazz, my pile of women's magazines beside the sofa; looking through my address book; pressing the memory numbers on my phone to see who answers; emptying the pewter-grey pots I bought years ago in Wales where I keep all my hairgrips, paperclips, stray earrings and darning needles, and the concert tickets from Stevie Wonder that Zack took me to. I imagine him lifting the lid of my potpourri jar and stirring up the petals with his fingers. He'll turn the pages of my calendar and read the scribbled notes I make for each day, then probe through the contents of my basketwork frog, where I stuff all receipts, trying to work out what I've bought in the last year. I see him discovering the photo album hidden under the middle sofa cushion, looking at the gaps on most of the pages, where Zack used to be. I know he'll see the top shelf of my bookcase and guess—without looking—that the titles with their spines back to front are books I'm ashamed of owning—like the *Story of 'O.'*

I listen in the bathroom doorway as I take off my clothes. I know nothing about him at all.

He shouts quietly up the stairs to me, as if he

knows I'm standing there, worrying. 'I'm looking at your videos.' Okay, I say, and turn on the shower. I fix up my hair and step into the bath and draw the curtain. There's a soap filled glove with rubber nipples for massage, and I use it vigorously on my buttocks and thighs. They ought to be smooth, I think. I scrub the rest of my body with a loofah glove, through which I sewed rough string myself, making lots of knots—I've always liked my skin to take a fair amount of punishment when I wash. Years ago, I remember, I had a rash all over my body which drove me crazy. I bought a small scrubbing brush, like the kind they use on the floor. That night I sat in the bath and used it on my legs and thighs until they bled. I felt high and breathless; all sexed-up afterwards. I used to ask Zack if he'd rub the bristles on my hair brush over my bottom when we were in bed. He'd do it, but not with any interest. I caught him reading a book once as he languidly scrubbed me.

I've always been very conscious, come to think of it, of touch, of skin. At primary school, when I was nine or ten, I remember the girl behind me drawing on my back and Jill, next to me, lifting my school blouse and writing messages on my skin with the blunt end of a pencil. On wet, dreary days, and especially during mental arithmetic with Mr Clark, the whole class would be in a trance; ranks of children drawing on each other's backs with rulers and fingers. Only the back row missed out, but as for me, sitting right at the front, I did nothing at all but enjoy it.

As I finish washing, he comes into the bathroom. It's force of habit, my not locking the door. Now, I wish I had. He pulls back the shower curtain and looks at me. 'You're red all over,' he says, touching my bottom, 'especially here.' As he speaks he unzips his trousers and pees into the bath, aiming deliberately for my red thighs. 'Don't,' I protest, but he simply pushes me around until my hands are on the wall and my back is turned to him, while he continues. 'I don't think you should get quite so bold with me, Rosy,' he says. The absence of threat in his voice is somehow very erotic. 'I think you should behave yourself. I can see I'm going to have to learn you.' It's such a *little* voice, the one he uses with me. It's special and obviously not the one he uses in the courts. He doesn't have to raise his voice to make me do what he wants. Yes, it's a little voice, deceptively casual and light. He might say—'hand me the newspaper, will you?' in the same tone he would say he was going to beat me.

As I stand with my back to him, he smacks me hard on the bottom, one, two, three, four, five, very hard. 'Remember,' he says, panting, 'it's spanks. Not smacks. Spanks. Okay?'

Okay.

He's looking at me critically with that smile on his face. Get out of the bath, he says. Do you have a razor? He's going to shave me. I tell him there's a pack of disposables in the cabinet and he searches through the empty talcs and half used cosmetics until he finds them. I stand on the bath mat and he kneels down in front of me, frowning at my pubic triangle. He tells me my hair is too

88

long, he'll have to cut it first with scissors. I point to my orange needlework scissors, lethally sharp, on the windowsill. He rubs my hair dry with a towel making it fluff. I look down at myself and feel mutinous. I don't want to be shaved. Carefully he cuts the springy curls down to a quarter of an inch. They fall onto the bath mat and he brushes them up with his fingertips into a little heap on the side. Then he dusts the remaining hair with talc and begins to shave the stubble. He's kneeling in front of me and I stare at the top of his head. Even though he is kneeling, I feel smaller.

I want to cry. He so calmly shaves away a part of me that's always been there. I feel violated and shocked. He taps my thighs and I widen them so he can reach in between my legs. He's very methodical, stretching the skin taut with his fingers. A tear drops onto the back of his hand. He looks up. 'It's not irreversible,' he says. 'It'll grow again.' I tell him I feel I've had an operation—that there's a vital part of me missing. He tells me he expects me to keep myself shaved smooth at all times.

When he's finished he gets a small mirror and shows me my new self. I look like a pre-pubescent girl. All the contours between my legs are visible. 'Touch yourself,' he says. My fingers go down and I rub the nude skin gently. He takes them and pushes my hand further, forcing my fingers up. 'Naughty,' he says. I blush. 'I'm wet from the shower,' I say. He grins and looks up at me. He wants to see me come, he says. Right here. Now. He wants to see me make myself come, so that he, still kneeling, can see it all. I argue with him and all he does is laugh. I don't want him to take his belt off to me, do I? I'm not that crazy? Go on, he says, I've had a helluva day at work. He wants some entertainment.

This is something I've never done in front of anyone. I'm not sure I can do it, with his eyes and his mouth inches from my body, watching me in such a calculated way. But I try, and I shame myself. I masturbate slowly, slipping my fingers over my clitoris and then down and back again. I widen my legs. I cease to care about feeling self-conscious. I begin to move my hips. I can hear my excited breathing. He watches me toss my head back, my fingers going round and round on the button. Then, suddenly, he yanks my hands away and pulls me to him. He sits down on the bathroom stool and jerks me down abruptly across his lap. He's lucky the bathroom's not too cramped to cope with this kind of activity. He grabs the wooden bathbrush and uses it on my bottom. I find myself writhing and kicking out with my legs almost hitting the sink with my head. I find myself gasping, pleading. Coming. . . .

When it's over he sprinkles talc on my bottom. It feels cool, as if he is blowing on my hot skin. He smooths it in circles and talks to me in a very quiet voice. I am aware, against my thigh, of his erection. Every few seconds it jumps. I turn my head and look at him. 'Won't you?' I say.

His fingers are exploring between my legs, making me squirm again.

'You're disgusting,' he says. 'You ought to

learn some self–control. I'll teach you, Rosy. I can see you need that.' Abruptly, he tips me onto the floor and while I struggle to get up he ties my hands loosely behind my back with the belt of my cotton kimono—the one he ripped on Saturday night.

When I was thirteen some older boys from the village tied my wrists behind me with binder-twine. They pushed me into a shallow stream where we all played and taunted me because I couldn't climb out. The moment now, when he pulls my wrists together, I feel slightly sick. I tense up. He hasn't tied me tightly—I can slip my hands out if I want. For a moment he watches me. 'You can free yourself,' he says, 'but I don't want you to. Will you play this little game with me?' I nod, but he takes my assent for granted. He tells me to roll over, get up, but stay on my knees. No—I mustn't free myself to do it, I must keep my hands behind my back. He sits down on the edge of the stool, legs apart. When I make it to my knees I notice his erect penis against the civi-lized background of grey pin-stripe suiting. He beckons me forward and I shuffle on my knees until I'm between his legs. He takes hold of my head and pushes me down until the tip of his penis touches my lips, and without a protest from me, passes through them.

It suddenly seems crazy, but I realize I've never done this before with Zack. Seven years and no variation? It can't be!

His hands rest on either side of my head, com-ing over my cheeks and under my jaw. As he enters my mouth he pushes my head down until I feel the length of him touching the back of my throat. My eyes water and I gag. He lifts my head up sharply, waits for me to recover and guides me down again, this time not as far. 'I can see I'll have to teach you, Rosy,' he says through his teeth.

He's panting now as he slips in and out of my mouth. I can feel the muscles of his thighs twitch. My lips cannot comprehend the size of him. I don't know if I should let him slide over my teeth, or try to curl my lips over them in case I graze him. He has no foreskin, and as I curl my tongue around the naked ridge, he gasps and throws back his head, gripping mine tightly with his hands. Then he pulls back on the stool until only the knob fills my mouth, and he moves it in and out rapidly, several times. I wonder what I will do when it happens. I think I'll throw up. But before then he pulls out completely and sits back, breathing hard. His eyes are closed. I realize I want him to come now, and blind my eyes. I want to pay back the debt. His breathing cools and he looks at me. We'll continue another time, he says, when he can teach me properly. His face is flushed. He grins. I know I did okay. He says it'll be very difficult to go through this evening with a perpetual hard-on. How's that for self-control, eh?

I stand up naked in front of him and I want him to kiss me, badly. He knows I do, so he slips the knot from my wrists, kisses them and turns away, flicking talc from his trousers.

Five minutes later I'm having the novel experience of stockings guided up my legs by a man. In films it's always the other way around—if you get one stocking off, you're home. He's making a mess of it and laughing at himself. He can't get the seams straight. He slides the silk up and down many times before getting it right. Then, with a grunt of satisfaction, he fastens them to the silk suspenders. I can't stop laughing. It seems the funniest thing to be dressed by him. Dammit, he says, he can dress himself without any trouble— why is it so complicated to hang clothes on me? I think how ridiculous he looks, holding out the knickers and telling me to put my left leg, then my right, into them, only to find they're back to front. He stops, watches me clap my hand over my mouth and my body fold up with giggles, and he turns away to hide his amusement. I poke him in the ribs and he laughs outright. I want to do something very sacrificial at that moment. He laughs and holds me around my waist, running his hands up and down the bare thigh above my stocking tops. Somehow I get into the dress and I dance around the room, wiggling my arse as he tries to zip me up at the side. He says I'll ruin him; he'd never defend me in court even though my crime is I'm only a middling cock-sucker.

The small box he bought from the car while I showered contains a pair of black suede shoes with a rosette of soft leather on the vamp and four inch heels. They fit. He says he remembered my size when I took off my sandals the day he massaged me. I can't walk in these, I tell him, but I try. I

93

look like a tart, he says, as I sway in front of him.

I smear lipstick on my mouth and brush my hair. He steps back and looks at me, enjoying my embarrassed excitement. I have the face of a nun and the body of a whore, he says. He goes into the hall and searches through my coats, coming back with a short grey jacket. I am not allowed to take my handbag. Nothing. We leave the house and he locks the door, putting my keys in his trouser pocket.

We drive into the city. There is a rose on my seat and a white card edged with gold underneath it. It says simply, 'My love's like a red, red, Rose.'

He takes me to a high-class Indian restaurant. We have drinks downstairs in the bar, sitting on high cane stools. He orders Campari for me and a draught beer for him. The decor is pink and grey, with large brass-framed prints of the English in India on the walls. Cool white fans cut the air above us. There are tall plants—not fake plastic—everywhere. We order from the menu. He asks for a chicken madras—extra hot. I stick to a milder korma. The waiter departs and I tell him I can't drink Campari with curry. 'If you don't want it,' he says, sliding his hand up my arm and speaking very quietly, 'spill it on the carpet.' I look down. The carpet is a pale pink. I don't think, instead I find myself doing exactly as he suggests. 'A half of Bass,' he says to an excessively polite waiter in a white jacket.

The restaurant is upstairs. As we go up he

watches me in the mirrors that line the staircase. I can see his eyes are fixed on my thighs. My stocking tops are visible as the dress rises with every step I take. He asks for a table near the huge glass window that looks into the kitchens. Behind the glass, like an actor on stage, a well-built chef in uniform skewers naans into the tandour in front of him. We watch as he slaps chapattis between his palms. The sound makes me blush. It reminds me of having my bottom smacked—spanked.

I watch him suffer with the Madras. We don't talk much. He adds extra chilli pickle to the same and eats breathlessly and at great speed. It's like a masochistic impulse he can't control. He finishes well before me and watches me eat while he chews on raw onion rings onto which he has smeared a large quantity of pickle. He says, 'Are you enjoying yourself, Rosy?' as if I had better be. I tell him I think curries are antisocial because for the last ten minutes I've seen his face screwed up as if he's in pain. I tell him he's outrageous and I hate the way he makes me do things. He scoffs and crams a piece of hot onion in my mouth.

'I'm not making you do anything,' he says, 'that you don't already want to do—deep down.'

'What about the Campari?' I say.

He smiles. 'Your hand didn't slip?'

It's 9:30 and we're drinking coffee in the small lounge off the main dining area. We're having brandy. Suddenly, there's a commotion behind us—scraping chairs, determined feet and hissing voices. 'V—,' a woman's voice says behind us.

It stuns me with its hostility. A dark haired woman wearing a red crepe jumpsuit marches up to him as he lounges opposite me in the lizard-striped chair, and looks down at him. Her right hand rests combatively on her waist. She repeats his name and flashes a look at me. A withering, jealous look, from a small, sharp face—very tanned—that has premature wrinkles fanning out from the corners of her eyes. 'I'm sorry,' she says to me in a voice as hard as chipped ice, and a smile to match. And she turns back to look at him. She's been trying to see him for weeks—and what about the money in lieu of her share of the car? She knows how clever solicitors are at tying things up. She'd like to get it settled before she moves.

He sighs and there's a very long pause before he says anything. I notice the smile on his face is mechanical. All the quizzical amusement it usually exhibits is gone. I look at his chest and his breathing is short and shallow. I move, offering to get up. In the quietest voice he tells me to sit down. He tells *her* to, in the nicest possible way, go fuck herself. I don't believe he's said it, and for a moment, neither does she. Her face darkens with anger and I think she's about to hit him. I have a sudden vision of him with a bloody nose. 'I'll go to the bar,' I say into the silence, getting up once more. She looks me up and down with sarcasm in her eyes and turns on her heels. Her words to me as she goes make me sink down into the chair. 'No, honey,' she says, 'you stay with him. Perhaps you're the type who enjoys being slapped about.'

We sit still for several minutes, not talking. I feel the blood rush to my face, then drain away. 'Was that your wife?' I ask at length.

'No,' he says, 'that was my ex-wife.'

He pays for the meal and we leave. I feel the other woman's eyes follow us as we walk across the restaurant floor. When we get outside he maneuvers me into a darkened doorway and puts his arms around me. He's upset and trying to lose himself in kisses. 'I want to fuck you Rosy,' he says, over and over.

We go through two red lights on the way back. He says, what the hell, the night's not over, and drives into the seedy heart of H—. At the end of the main street are cellar night clubs, gambling dens and strip-joints. He says we'll call in at the Tabasco club. I tell him he'll get his car stolen. He grins. It'll get him out of paying his ex-wife. The walls are lined with red flocked wallpaper as we go down the carpeted stairs into the club. The place reeks of stale smoke. There's a black bouncer on the door talking with two other guys. The bouncer wears black and has a white cummerbund around his middle which isn't at all clean. He looks at us both and gives us the no-no. One of the other guys recognizes V and draws us both through the door, crying 'Hey man, how you doin''.

It's a small room, not much bigger than my living room at home. It's dark except for the bar lights at one end of the room. At the other end is a small area for musicians and a dancing area big enough for only a dozen couples cheek to cheek.

97

As we get a drink a black DJ is setting up his stuff. You oughta come here about eleven, says V's friend, it don't start to get lively till then. I sit on a tall bar stool and listen to them. They talk mainly about the Court and the police. Occasionally, V leans over to me and slides a hand up underneath my dress. Then, just after eleven, the people—the clubbers—start to come in. They bring with them a strange air of excitement that filters through to us—there's trouble on the streets. We ask, but no one seems to know exactly what's happening. Someone says there's been a drug bust. The DJ puts on some heavy funk but nobody dances.

I tell him I'm scared. I feel trapped in the basement. Gangs of riot-crazed people could pour down the stairs at any moment—police charging after them with batons, tear gas, hitting out indiscriminately. I imagine being dragged upstairs and pushed into a van. I tell him I want to go home. I don't think he understands how I feel. He's lighthearted, jokey. His manner unnerves me. He says, okay, we'll go, but he wants to find out more about the trouble. Outside I plead with him to take me back straight away. He actually laughs at me, at my fear. I know I'm beaten: I've got no money for a taxi and my keys are deep in his trouser pocket. I'm stuck with him, and he's crazy.

Two guys outside the club talk to him while I hang around miserably. Then he grabs my hand and takes me to the back entrance, where he tells me to wait among the rubbish bins and graffiti, while he moves his car, parking it next to the fire escape from the building next door. It's hidden from the road by the bins. He must trust these people, I think. He must have friends among the fringe.

He says we're going to walk through H—. It's safer. He doesn't want to drive down a street and have the car seized by rioters and set alight in the middle of the road. He says we'll be better protected if we walk among them. I say he's mad and I hit him on the arm. He seems to be all fired up by the violence in the air.

It's a warm night, the sort of night when things happen. People never lose their tempers in the rain. We go quickly down a road leading away from clubland and the main street. Half a mile away in front of us is a glow in the sky. I don't notice it at first until he points it out to me—I think it's just streetlamps. Out of the darkness behind us three fire engines roar past and the street becomes a muddle of flashing lights. They veer down a side street and, minutes later, are followed by police vans and motorbikes. Before long we come across groups of people standing on the street. House windows are open. People look out. There are shouts ahead, bottles smashing, the revving of engines. The whole suburb creeps out onto the streets, watching, the younger ones getting infected by the violence—picking up stones and broken masonry from the gutters and hiding them in their pockets. No one takes any notice of us. In fact, they're almost friendly. If we're here, we must be okay, they reason. We begin to see police in the shadows—a brick smashes a street lamp and

99

they become just sinister shapes, their helmets and riot shields picking up light from the glow of burning buildings fifty yards away. The street is running with water and V pulls me down a side road where we cut across behind the burning shops and emerge near the heart of the trouble. We hover about twenty yards from the junction to see flames leaping from a row of shops which form the center of this district. In front of us, running past, are scattered gangs of youths hurling missiles. It's chaos. We don't see any police because their vehicles have been effectively barricaded by burning, overturned cars. I watch as a group of about eleven youths overturn a car at the head of the junction. Within minutes it's a fireball. Figures run behind the flames like they're dancing around some huge bonfire party. There are shouts, dogs barking and burglar alarms going off one after another. Down our side street three shops have been set alight and the fire brigade is trying to put out the blaze. They get attacked by bricks. There's a crowd around us and we flow with it. We are the watchers.

We lean against the wall on the opposite side of the road, as near as seems safe. A drunk Irish woman stands next to me, gibbering in a monologue. She wears a low cut dress and there are bruises, like love-bites down the inside of her arms and across the top of her breasts. All she does is talk and shiver. Her bare arms glisten with sweat in the fire-light. She leans forward and vomits between her legs, stands up, sniffs and walks past us, her head held high and her worn heels scraping along the pavement. She mutters something about a stolen handbag.

The fire is out now in the shops and the fire truck moves on. The people move in like vultures. I feel I'm one of them even though I'm only watching. I feel I'm part of the crowd-consciousness that causes a riot. A young black throws a brick through the only unbroken window and there's laughter. He runs across the road and into the newsagents which lies in between the shop selling baby clothes and a greengrocers. He comes out again with three boxes of cigars in his back trouser pocket. Someone cries, 'Get us twenty Rothmans, will you?' A young girl with a baby in a pushchair rushes across the street with her friend. We all watch them, wonder what they will do in front of us all. The friend goes into the drapers and stuffs a carrier bag full of disposable nappies and baby clothes, while the mother and baby wait anxiously outside, looking out for the police. They run off down the pavement, the push-chair wheels roaring as they speed over the cracks. I look at V. He has a cheroot between his lips and he's chewing the end. It's not lit. I want to say something—ask him what he thinks of the scene we're observing but I can't. Although it's calm now, and everybody's friendly, I can't make any moral judgement, no matter how trivial. If I do, I'll break this queer no-man's-land of trust in the face of crime. I may get attacked for it. I watch V's face, profiled in darkness beside me and I wonder what thoughts are going through his head. Does he feel, with his expensive suit and his wallet full of money and credit cards, that we're no better or worse than the people all around us, who are only taking what they need? Perhaps he feels the shame and the guilt too.

A middle-aged woman comes out of the newsagents with a can of chilli beans. One tin of beans. She holds them up to us all as though she's just won first prize in a competition. I feel like crying and applauding her. I don't know why. A black guy takes a hand of bananas from the smashed shop front of the greengrocers, balances them on his shoulders, and shuffles his feet around in a dance. I whisper in V's ear, 'Where are the police?' He turns to me and grins before kissing me very sexily on the mouth. It seems an obscene thing to do under the circumstances. He asks the guy next to him about the cause of the trouble. It's a drug bust, the police lose their cool and start hitting. An old black lady gets hit and falls bleeding to the ground. I listen and it doesn't seem possible. How can one incident lead to all this? But I can feel the energy in the air, ready to snap and bite each one of us, including me. It's like being on a high, experiencing some atavistic feeling that civilization has deprived us of and pretends it away under the surface of our lives.

A white Audi cruises up the street from the opposite direction to the trouble. There's suddenly music, heavy reggae music, loud and pulsating, from the open car windows. There are cheers—hey, man, this is a party! Go for that sound, man! Two black guys get out of the car. They wear lightweight expensive suits. One has gold chains

102

around his neck and large coin rings on his knuckles. I can tell they're not from this area. The crowds here are small fry. They haven't the confidence to do what these guys are doing. We watch as they walk calmly into the newsagents and upstairs into the living quarters above it. Minutes later they come out carrying a large color television between them which they load into the boot of the Audi. The family who live there come out of the crowd and the old Grandmother collapses onto her two daughters, sobbing and crying, 'not that, not that!'

Someone shoves an open sweet jar under my nose, full of lemon sherbets. I recognize the guy as the one who sold me beer at the carnival. He grins. I don't know what to do but grin back. The sugar glistens on the sweets in the jar but I shake my head, then change my mind and dip my fingers into the neck of the jar. I'm eating a looted sherbet. V notices and shakes his head disapprovingly. 'Naughty girl,' he says.

The guy offers him a sweet but V declines. The sherbet jar makes its way down the whole line of us leaning against the wall. In the street some people are dancing to the music. Then the two in suits get back into their car and drive away. The music receeds eerily. I feel punch-drunk and lightheaded. It's not real. I can't get it into my head that it's real.

Commotion—lights in a line across the road way back. Lights advancing; shouts. Lights drawing nearer. Tension suddenly explodes as three police transits, followed by two behind, drive slowly towards us. In front of them are a tight line of police in riot gear, hiding behind their shields. The lights are so bright it's difficult to make out the line in front of them. It's a shock to realize they're men, coming for us.

We find ourselves fronting an angry crowd now, armed with half bricks and bottles, some filled with rags and petrol. It gets ugly. Missiles go over our heads and I duck close to the wall, my hands around my neck. There's not time to scream. To my left is an alleyway between houses and V pushes me down it. We look out as the bricks fly past. The Irish woman has returned and is hit on the shoulder. We see her go down in the place where I had been standing.

The houses either side of the alley are boarded up, empty. He finds a broken door and we go inside to the sound of petrol bombs exploding in the road. We hold each other. I find I'm giggling. He pushes me against a wall and lifts up my dress. He lifts me. My legs wrap round his waist and my hands cling round his neck as he pushes me higher against the wall. I slide down on him and he fucks me, shouting and crying out when he comes.

Five minutes later we're back on the street running, caught between the police and the people. The lights are nearly upon us now, the great headlamps behind them making the shadows sharp. We see visored helmets behind shields, advancing toward us in the blinding glare. The bricks start flying over my head. He pushes me toward the lights, to the line of faceless men behind the

104

shields. It parts to let us through, because we're white and he's wearing a suit.

I look round as soon as we're safely through and I see the police hitting the people with their white batons, and I feel sick.

He takes me home then, and stays with me, because I can't stop my body shaking.

7.

One day after half term he meets me in college. I've just had some sharp words with Zack in the corridor and, to show my annoyance, I run on ahead of him, letting the door slam in his face.

It's funny how different people look when you see them where you don't expect to. It just shows me how much of our lives we live in compartments; boxes, that don't know how to intercommunicate. So when I see V coming towards me, swinging his jacket over his arm, I have this puzzled feeling— yes, I've seen you somewhere, I know you, don't I? But I don't recognize you in the context of this cold, dim tunnel. He comes nearer, does a few skips up to me and grins. 'Rosy,' he says. I feel quite shocked seeing him there, and because I'm at work, I don't show him how pleased I really am. I ask him what he's doing and am not happy about the frosty little edge to my voice.

'I finished early. I thought I'd look you up.'

I tell him I'm about to start a class. He'll have to go away. He says he'd like to stay around and listen outside the door when I'm teaching. I ignore the remark and ask how he managed to get past the security guards. How many terrorists do I know, he says, who have such a good tailor? He kisses me with lips that are hot.

I've forgotten about Zack. Zack who had the door slammed in his face half a minute ago, for telling me he's going to marry Carol. He comes round the corner and catches us in the act of kissing. I see the expression on his face as he walks past—it's one of fury. He goes all pompous and clutches his folders close to his chest as if to say how important he is. His crepe-soled shoes squeak on the polished floor, making him ridiculous. I stare after him, turn to V and giggle. Zack hears me and stops. I was wondering how long it would take before his curiosity won out. He turns in a squeaky circle and marches back to us. V is in the process of lighting a small cheroot. It's an act of effrontery, I'm sure. You must be Zack, he says. Aha . . . well. . . .

Zack slaps his folder against his chest. 'And you're the solicitor? Yes. . . .' He holds out his hand. V takes it by the tips of the fingers, like a woman. It's deliberate, I know.

'I hope,' Zack says, 'you're looking after Rose.'

V snorts. 'Like you did?' he says, very quiet, dangerously funny.

Zack's disdainful smile freezes. I can't believe

it—he's threatened. 'Have you known her long?' he says.

'Long enough.'

'And you live here, do you?'

V nods and breathes smoke out through his nostrils.

'Well,' Zack says, beaten, 'If I ever need any free legal advice, I'll know where to come.' And with that he makes to go.

I'm wearing the high-heels V bought me, to get accustomed to them. It's a mistake to wear them to college. The floors are polished to a glass shine. As Zack moves away he reached out and touches my arm in a stupid possessive gesture. I step back to avoid it and my shoes slide from under me and I go down on the floor. Instinctively, I put out my arm, fall awkwardly on it, and the next second, the world spins in pain. I hear Zack and V arguing above me. Their faces seem a long way off. The last thing I hear before I go unconscious is the two of them blaming each other for what has happened.

When I come to, I'm in V's car. The pain in my elbow makes me cry out. I slip away again. I get to the hospital and nurses help me. Behind me, I can hear Zack. He must have followed us in his car. How funny, says a little voice in the back of my head—removed from everything—they're fighting over me. I've never had that happen before.

I don't remember much, apart from the pain and the feeling that the hinge on my elbow is working the wrong way. When I come to, I'm in a hospital

bed and my arm is in plaster. A nurse tells me
I've dislocated my elbow and had to be put out in
order to realign it. I'm not really aware of anything until the evening.

The first person I see that I recognize is Zack.
I hear him tell the staff nurse he's my husband. I
try to get up off the bed and protest, but it doesn't
seem worth it. He's bought me a large basket of
fruit—big enough for the whole ward—which I
don't feel like eating right now. I switch off when
I hear all his platitudes. In fact, I'm laughing inside, but the sound doesn't have the energy to
make it to my mouth. Zack takes my hand and
starts stroking the plaster very gently. He's apologizing so much I wish he'd shut up. He's making
it sound like a confessional, only I end up feeling
guilty. I close my eyes and when I open them
again I see V standing on the other side of the
bed, with the largest bouquet of flowers I've ever
seen in my life. They don't look like the sort of
flowers you buy in a florist's—all stiff stemmed
and no scent, smelling of marble tombs—these
flowers are sun daisies and buddleia blossom, hy-
drangea heads and bourbon roses; agapanthus,
marigolds, michaelmas daisies, asters and cape lil-
ies. The bouquet is so enormous I can hardly see
his body behind it.

'Where did you get them?' I ask, noticing the
cellophane wrapping around them and the extrava-
gant red satin bow. He lays the flowers on the bed
and leans over me to whisper in my ear. 'From
the people of H—,' he laughs. I wonder what he
means. (Later he tells me he collected them from

109

people's gardens. Did you steal them, I ask? Now, would a law abiding man do such a thing, he says?) He tells me that he took them all to a florist and she arranged them in a bouquet for him. He catches Zack's stiff expression and stands up, giving him a slightly mocking smile. A nurse taps him on the shoulder. They haven't enough vases to put them in, she says, dismayed. I unwrap the flowers and hide the small envelope inside them under the bedclothes. He lets me admire them before separating some blooms from the rest and passing them to the nurse. He'll take the others to my house and fill it with flowers. He looks at Zack as he says he's got my keys in his pocket.

Zack looks murderous. I don't feel guilty in the least just now about having someone else. What is he doing here, anyway, I ask myself? He left me for Carol. He wants to fuck up my life, that's all.

I watch them both as they each talk to me, ignoring the other's existence. Zack's anger is almost a preening display. Parts of the flibbert have rubbed onto him—it's said you take on the traits of those with whom you live. He'd better start manicuring his nails. I wonder if she knows he's here. How would she feel if she saw him stroking my plaster. I look at the other people in the ward. They're all watching with interest and, in one or two cases, amusement. It's a play, I think, or a satirical revue, as they quick-fire lines at the audience, which is me. I sink down beneath the covers and let them get on with it.

I'm trying to guess who's bought me a nightie,

because all I have on at the moment is a hospital gown. Right on cue V produces a small bag from his jacket pocket and a short cream nightdress with thin straps slides out onto the bed. Zack reddens and looks disgusted. Now you're getting a dose of your own medicine, I think cruelly. I remember what I felt like when he said he was leaving me for Carol. A little maliciousness right now feels good.

Later, when they've both gone and the ward is quiet, I take out the white envelope from under the bedclothes. It's warm with the heat of my body. Of course—it has to be: a poem. It reads,

"What thing is love? For sure love is a thing.

It is a prick, it is a sting,

It is a pretty, pretty thing;

It is a fire, it is a coal,

Whose flame creeps in at every hole . . .'

I find myself blushing. He wants to remind me of sex while I'm lying in a hospital bed? It seems out of place to bring sex in here. I feel uncomfortable as if I've come from another planet with embarrassing values that have no place. He's reminding me of another life, a life before today. The compartments don't communicate. I think and ask myself—is sex something I don like a coat when I'm with him, or is my sex a part of me, actually my soul? Am I merely responding to him? What, I wonder, *is* really mine?

My arm is now out of plaster. It doesn't feel as though it belongs to me—it's an awkward hinge which doesn't work properly. I have to visit the

111

physiotherapist in the hospital for exercises. It all seems terribly slow. That weekend, he decides to come and stay with me. He says I need someone to make a fuss of me. He's going to entertain me, cook for me. I feel a little scared. I think, I don't want him to get intimate with my home. If he leaves me, if we finish, I'll still see him in here, touching my things. I'll smell him where he's sat on my sofa or slept in my bed. And I'll have to live with it, every day.

I feel a kind of helplessness. He's beginning to take over my life so that I don't have time to think. When I'm alone I find it hard to work out where I'm going. Every thought runs back to him. I'm having to let go of the past and it frightens me. I listen to Pat Metheny and it doesn't make me cry anymore. I used to think about Zack and I, walking along a Devon beach together, when I heard it, but now it's different. The music has a clarity, uncluttered by my emotion. It's a new experience. I realize I'm having to give up my self pity and I feel a bit miffed about doing so. Do I want this man to change me, I ask myself? And then I think, it's me—I'm doing the changing all on my own. He's just the one with the key.

He comes to the house at nine on Saturday morning and I open the door as he parks in front of the garage. There's music playing and I ask what it is. 'Art Pepper,' he says and flips the tape out of the machine and throws it to me. He's wearing black cords and a white short-sleeved shirt. His dark curls are still damp from a shower. I notice that his chin and cheeks, usually smooth, have a dark shadow of stubble on them. He slams the car door, bounces towards me in his white trainers and stops about nine inches from my face to look at me. He's amused by my scrutiny.

'Have you missed me?' he asks.

I nod.

He comes past me, grabs my arms and gives me a kiss on my forehead. It's restrained, for him. I'm aware though that underneath there is fire in his blood, held back only by an effort of supreme self–control. I figure he's got something planned, for later.

'Hey!' he says, 'you've got your arm back!' I'm wearing a blue dolman sweater and he doesn't notice till then that my arm is out of plaster. I tell him it's stiff and won't straighten properly. As I talk I pull up the sleeve and show him. Suddenly, I start to cry—I feel it'll never mend. I feel so frustrated. He closes the front door and guides me into the living room where he sits down on the sofa and pulls me on his lap. I curl up there, tucking my legs up beside me on his knees, and he rocks me back and forth like a child. I cry even louder. It seems I can't cope with what his tenderness is doing to my emotions. I continue to find lots of things to cry about. Lots of self-pitying images of Zack come into my mind and I feast on them, milk them for what they're worth. I am small and frightened and I'm crying my heart out. I use him—his body warmth, his soft crooning voice, his arms hugging me tight—to release feelings I can't put into words. I'm grateful and I let

113

the tears go on until they stop of their own accord. He's not frightened of my tears. Zack was.

'You'll feel better now,' he says, 'now you've got rid of that old rope.'

I tell him I haven't cried like that for a long time. He says I'm beginning to thaw out. It's good. My emotions are coming back to me. He eased me off his lap and makes me lie down on the sofa. He covers me with an old blanket and puts two cushions under my head. Then he leaves me, and I hear him clattering among my kitchen drawers, humming to himself every so often. I fall asleep.

I wake up forty minutes later to find him sitting on the floor beside the sofa, legs crossed like a buddha. He's drinking coffee with a soft smile on his face. As I open my eyes, I see an expression in his that I'm too sleepy to interpret. His stillness as he stares at me is unnerving. I ask how long he's been there. Since he found out I have no onions and absolutely no spices, he says. He's going to make me a curry for lunch. We'll have to go shopping. I roll off the sofa and he pushes my arms above my head, maneuvering his body on top of me, squashing the air from my lungs. I feel that he's hard. 'All you've got is stale curry powder,' he says, licking my face with broad strokes of his tongue. 'I'm going to show you how to do it properly.'

We take the bus to the top of H——'s main street. We walk down past the shops—past the greengrocers, spilling vegetables to the edge of the pavement so there's barely enough room to walk; past

the many sweet centers. He goes into the Shah-
Bagh and buys me two sticky jelabi's and a small
polystyrene container with two gulab jamun in
syrup. Most of the shopkeepers here are Asian, as
are most of the shoppers. We must look an odd
couple, I think: him in the grey coat with the velvet collar, and trainers on his feet—me in a rather
tight skirt and heels. We go past shops I have
known for years, yet with him they seem new,
exciting. Every other one seems to be a super-
market-greengrocers. Vegetables are outside under
awnings. The women rake through large boxes of
garlic, ginger root and chillies, their bangles slapping, and they fill brown bags with them. There
are fresh karela and curry leaves, gingko nuts,
coconuts, okra, aubergines, loquats, courgettes
and peppers, fresh coriander in pungent green
bunches and clover-like fenugreek—even though
the regular season for most of them has gone.
There are also plantain and sugar cane, yams of
all shapes and sizes that are sliced off with a ma-
chete knife by the pound, and boxes of stinking
snappers just inside the door. And it's all so cheap
here.

As we walk along people acknowledge us. I
know students from college, and V gets accosted
frequently by young blacks and middle-aged Asians,
who have come to him, at one time or another,
for legal help.

He propels me into a crowded shop near the
college. He selects vegetables from the piled-high
boxes outside and puts them into bags, handing
them to me while I watch. Two Asian ladies gig-

115

gle as he examines four chillies and drops them in the bottom of a large paper bag. They buy them, as they always do, by the bagful. I am amazed at myself for being so ignorant. Zack never liked me to cook curries at home. He hated the smell that lingered afterwards. He was always careful not to eat garlic before meetings at college. Right now, I see V peel a small clove with his teeth and chew it.

We go inside the shop to buy spices in large plastic bags: cinnamon bark, dhania, jeera, haldi and more. He grins at me and then at the shop's owner whom he knows. 'It's Jasvir,' he says to me and points to small boxes on a shelf behind the counter, at the fine silver leaf-work.

'Aidi ki kimath hai?' he asks, and I stare at him in amazement.

'What are you saying?' I hiss at his side, suddenly possessed by the desire to giggle.

'Punjabi,' he says. 'I went to classes.'

'What?' I fall onto his shoulder, laughing.

'Aidi ki kimath hai?' he repeats, and the shop-keeper, all smiles in my direction, raises both hands in a gesture of apology.

'Five pounds nearly,' he says, showing us his palm.

'What?' V says, grinning at Jasvir, *'Choor!'*

They both laugh as V hands over his basket, and talk in a mixture of English and Punjabi. V tells him he's buying all the spices because he's going to cook me a real curry. He puts his arm around my waist and draws me to his side in a

116

gesture both possessive and sexual. Jasvir's eyes gleam as he looks at us.

'I'm going to give her the best,' V says, squeezing me, and he adds, *'Anu te mai khoosh kee lena ya.'*

Jasvir laughs throatily and he looks down for a second, then up at me, a sly expression on his face.

'Uno te pata ya be nahi?' he says to V, running his tongue over his lips.

I look from one to the other. I think I'll wait until we get outside before I ask V for a translation. Already I can feel a blush rising up my neck. He pays for the shopping and Jasvir smiles at him all the while as if they're sharing a private joke.

When we are ten yards from the shop I pounce on V excitedly and ask him for an explanation. He won't tell me at first, but teases me. 'What did you say?' I shriek, laughing. He smiles and looks at the sky.

'I told him I was going to make you very happy.' He looks at me and grins. 'You'll enjoy what I make for you.'

'You didn't say that,' I counter.

'I did. And he said simply, does she know or not? What's wrong with that?'

I pretend to be angry. I say I think he told Jasvir he was going to give me a good fuck. How could he! V strides out in front of me, while I run to catch him up. 'Well?' I say crossly, 'Isn't that what you meant?'

'It could well be,' he answers and slips across the road at the lights before I can hit him.

Half an hour later he's finished his shopping and we walk back across the park. He carries two bags and I, one. I don't know why we can't take the bus, but it's his idea, the walk. I know if I disagree with him too much, I'll suffer for it later on. I'm not sure I don't want to argue with him on purpose. We cross the football pitches and cut down through the trees. The chestnuts are almost nude, their leaves just a mass of flame-tints crunching underfoot. I kick through them like a child, enjoying the rustling noise around my legs. Then I ask him why he learnt Punjabi. It seems odd to me. He tells me he works one day a week at H— Law Center. Most of his clients are Asian. He finds the language a great help. 'Even if they speak another dialect,' he says, 'they know I'm going to take their problem seriously.' He sees people who have immigration difficulties and tells me about a woman he saw last week who has one child and wants her husband to come from India to live with her. It's like trading in lives he says— only brown skins here aren't worth all that much. He tells me about people he sees who have been unfairly dismissed at work because they don't speak much English, and can't understand that they have civil rights too. I didn't know, I say, thinking. 'Do you give your services free?'

'Yup.' He seems uncomfortable, or perhaps I'm reading him wrong, and he splashes ahead of me through the leaves. I don't know why I do it, and it's the wrong time to ask, but I find myself questioning him about his wife. I tell him I'm sorry for prying, and if he doesn't want to tell me

I'll accept it. What did she mean—I say the words carefully—by 'slapped about'?

He drops the carrier bags languidly where he stands and the contents of one bag spill out. Onions roll down the tarmac path among the leaves. He turns round in a circle and shrugs, not looking at me. The smile is gone.

Desperately I say it doesn't matter; I've no business, I could bite my tongue. Tears prick my eyes. I don't want to change things between us. Even if it's only a crazy dream which has to end, I don't want it to—not yet. He looks up and stares at me for a long time, his hands thrust deep into his coat pockets. I feel suddenly cold, wide open, raw. There is a space between us which I have made. I can't cross it and ask him to forgive me. It's been said.

When he speaks, he has difficulty choosing the words. He starts to say something, but his voice dies away. I see the muscles in his cheeks working and his jaw is clenched tight. He sighs lengthily.

'I guess someone else could tell you,' he says, in a dull, flat voice. 'I used to spank my wife.'

'Oh.' I look up. May the tree above me fall on my head.

'When she met this guy she filed for divorce.' He winces. 'I had an injunction served on me for violence. Unreasonable behavior, that's how she got rid of me.' He turns once again on his heels. 'I didn't beat her up,' he says, with a shrug.

I see him standing just past the tree I am underneath—dark, stone-silent, not even waiting for me to say something that'll make it okay again. I

119

know what he's thinking—what can I say? What would most women do now? Run? Is that what he thinks I'll do? Well, I might, just at this moment, but I wouldn't be running from him, but from myself and my own crippling jealousy. I shuffle towards him through the hump of leaves that separate us.

'Did she enjoy being spanked?' I ask.

He laughs incredulously, bitterly, and then it warms. 'Let's say she tolerated it. She didn't really like it.'

I give a fragile smile. How easily I spring to his defense! I think about the time, three hours ago, when he cradled me on his lap like a child. 'I think she's a cow,' I say. I look into his dark eyes. 'Will it change things between us?' He says he is the way he is. It won't change, unless I leave him. His smile returns. He knows, somehow, that I won't.

He's in my kitchen now, leaping about with a large cast iron frying pan in his hand while I watch him as I sit at the table. I've never seen anyone work so fast. I'm amazed he doesn't forget some vital ingredient. He sharpens my only cook's knife and sets to work chopping onions like a chef, never lifting the blade from the board. Soon they are reduced almost to pulp. He gets me to peel a whole head of garlic and then smashes each clove under the blade. While I prepare vegetables at the sink he drops spices into hot, pungent mustard oil. He dry roasts dhania and jeera in a small cast-iron pan and the delicious smell of burnt oranges fills the house. After the spices he adds the onion, garlic, and some of the fresh ginger pulp stirring it to make a paste. 'None of your fucking curry powder,' he tells me and proceeds to fry the vegetables in the pan. It's confusing—the speed at which he cooks—so after a while I leave him and listen to the tape he gave me when he arrived. He cooks in my kitchen and shouts at me from the stove. Do I know, he says, that Art Pepper once made a recording under the name Art Salt, because otherwise, he would have violated his recording contract? Do I know he was a crazy junkie, obsessed with his prick, quite happy to screw anything with a cunt? To hear him, I'd never believe it, would I? No, I wouldn't. The guy sounds heavenly. I'd call it spiritual. It just shows, V says, coming into the room, bouncing drumsticks around in a saucepan, that carnality is often the basis for genius, if not the cause. Had I heard about Mingus? Well, in his autobiography, it does nothing else but repeat the dimensions of his ten inch prick. V—you're spoiling my naive appreciation of the music, I say. I don't want to know about these musicians' hang-ups!

When the dishes are cooking he opens a beer and comes into the room, throwing himself down on the carpet. We have an hour to fill before lunch, he says. Now, how could we best use it?

He draws the curtains over the front windows and strips off his shirt. The smell of his sweat, mingled with the scent of soap makes me feel faint. I almost feel guilty about feeling this way.

121

He's the only man I've ever known, though, who makes me aware of the eroticism of shame. He undresses me carefully, being very gentle as he eases my stiff elbow out of my sweater and the blouse underneath. He examines it and kisses the bruises which are still there from the accident. He says, 'You think I'm going to be kind to you because of your poor old arm.' If I do, I'm very much mistaken. There are other areas of my body which aren't quite so sacrosanct. He tells me, as he unzips my skirt, he's thought of little else at night but beating my bottom with my hairbrush. It really turns him on just to think about it. Because the brush is mine, is so intimate to me after so many years, he sees it as something almost sacred. And being sacred in his eyes, he naturally wants to violate it. 'Well, Rosy,' he says, as he undoes my stocking, 'will you play this little game with me?' I pretend to give it some thought. He unhooks my bra and starts to play roughly with my breasts, squeezing and pumping them. He says what he's doing is 'conventional foreplay' and he hates it. Seeing my surprise, he goes on to explain. Sex, he says, has been civilized into a number of stages. You start by kissing, then progress to fondling the breasts. After the lady grows used to the idea, you carefully lower your attention, he says, to the thighs. Easy does it. The cunt is like a jewel. You have to be mighty cunning if you want to be allowed to even look at it. He says Alex Comfort and his *JOY OF SEX* is crap. All this politeness and consideration for the other partner is crap. He says he's going to whup me in a minute if I don't answer him.

Okay, I say.

That's the last time I'm going to ask your permission, he says.

He gets a stick-backed chair from the kitchen and places it in the middle of the room. I'm naked apart from my pants. He's still wearing his black cords. He tells me to go and fetch my hairbrush. I feel scared as I go out of the room. Something's bothering me. I feel I'm becoming an object for his desires. I'm not sure that I like it. For the first time, I'm really uneasy. Does it have anything to do with his disclosure in the park? It might. Now he's got that out of the way—and I didn't run off in horror—he might feel it's tantamount to my giving him permission to do anything he likes. Anything at all. Quietly I go upstairs for my hairbrush, and come down with it, turning the bristles over and over in my hand.

When I enter the room he's sitting on the chair with his arms folded, his legs slightly apart. He looks dark, serious. I feel a rush of panic. He beckons me forward until I'm standing in front of him and our knees touch. He wants me to listen to him for a minute. Up to now, he says, he's been consciously holding himself back. He's been restrained, playing it cool with me, showing me how much self-control he has. Now, he says, he's going to ease off the brakes. Would I lower my knickers, please? He takes the hairbrush from me and watches me as I roll the white cotton triangle down over my thighs. Every time he wants to fuck

123

me now, he continues, he's going to. He has a big appetite for sex. He doesn't think I realize that yet. Would I turn around, please, and bend over so he can admire the white purity of my buttocks, which in a minute are going to be red? I look at him fiercely but, as he says, it's only a game, so I do as he asks me. It is a game, isn't it? Do I know how many times he has masturbated in the past week for instance? No, I couldn't possibly. He starts to count on his fingers, then gives up. A man should never need to do that if he's got access to a woman he's crazy about. So, he's been considerate to me, hasn't he?

At this point I turn to face him and giggle nervously. I tell him I could interpret what he's just said as his actually denying me sex. It's a clever way to get me wanting it all the time. He smiles. I like that. I like the way I can make him smile when he's trying to be serious. It's reassuring. He pulls me nearer and runs his hands over my body. He has the audacity to pick up my knickers from the floor and smell them, making me blush.

The phone rings. He answers. It's Zack. 'She's fine,' he says briskly. 'What d'you want to know for?' I silently motion for the receiver and with a black look, he gives it to me.

Zack is creepily contrite. He's ringing to find out about my arm. I suspect he's really checking up on me. I hope he enjoyed hearing V's voice. Zack goes on and on. He says he's still very sorry about the accident. He says maybe I oughtn't to wear high heels if I can't walk in them properly. V takes the phone from me and says, very smoothly, that he's looking after me. He's sure Zack's got better things to do. They talk for a while longer. V's voice is taut and sharp. I turn away. I don't like the thought that Zack is pursuing me, but at the same time I guess I'm touched by his concern, even if I'm annoyed that I am.

When I turn round again V has finished speaking and is sitting back on the chair. I can see anger in his muscles. Before I can speak he grabs me, pulls me down across his lap and spanks me hard and fast. I cry out but he doesn't stop. I've never seen him like this before. He's talking to me in a voice no louder than a whisper and I close my eyes, listening to him between slaps. He tells me to say I want to be fucked. I resist, shake my head, tear my hair along the carpet. Damn him! He knows that I do! He says he'll make me cry. He begins to use the hairbrush on my bottom. It smarts like hell. I think of the Singh family next door. I imagine they're listening to this. I give in. 'I want to be fucked,' I say. Please, V, fuck me. He smacks the smooth wood down on my tender flanks even harder. He won't stop. What the hell is going to happen?

Somehow, somewhere, I reach a point in the pain when I begin to lose all my resistance. My will just departs. I start to cry at the loss—it's like losing my identity. The feeling is alien to me. I'm being pushed farther than I've ever experienced in my emotions. All kinds of feelings come up, one by one, all the little demons of my past life, and the pain seems to dissolve the power they once had over me. I plead with him and he throws the

125

hairbrush across the room and continues with his hand. I plead with him now, but I don't know if I want him to stop or to carry on. It's frightening. I've never been here before. Never felt myself surrender to anyone like this—in such depth. He stops suddenly and I slide off his lap onto my knees. I can hear myself making a queer noise, halfway between a sob and a gasp of adoration. I go between his trousered knees and look up. 'I love you,' I say.

He makes a little sound in his throat, a little suppressed cry of triumph. He stands up, kicks the chair, sending it flying across the room and takes off his trousers. Then he sits on the floor and tells me to sit on a cushion between his thighs, facing him, supporting myself like he is, on outstretched arms. I lower myself carefully onto his penis. We are both shaking. He moves back and forth, throwing his head back. I see ecstasy on his dark, handsome face. It is then I notice the handset on the carpet beside the phone. I look into V's eyes, at the darkness there. As I feel him move inside me, as we move together, I find I cannot sustain the thought that Zack may have heard everything for more than the merest fraction of a second. His eyes seem to shut themselves off from me as he comes. I feel his body shiver and I come too, just watching him. 'Maithuna,' he says, dropping his head on his chest. We sit there joined for—I don't know how long—and I feel him grow again. This time he withdraws to turn me over, with rough animal hands. He gets the chair, hauls me up over the back of it. He fucks me from

126

behind, letting go, feeling his maleness. And when he comes this time, it's in a crazy, noisy, possessed kind of way, like he's trying to take me inside himself, and keep me there.

I don't remember who put the receiver back on the phone. I don't want to. If Zack heard—well, that's tough. There's nothing I can do about it now.

He feeds me the choicest bits of vegetables and chicken from his curry. It's delicious. We do silly things, like pass a long finger of okra back and forth between our mouths. He eats a whole chilli in front of my eyes and I watch him cry and laugh and his face go red. He rushes out, rubbing his eyes, making it worse. I realize my feelings for him have gone past the point where I can let him go. I know I'll do anything to have him stay. It's serious—he doesn't say he loves me, or anything like that. There are no promises. I tell myself if he goes I'll accept it. I'll put it down to a wild, crazy affair. But now I know if he does go, I'll be devastated, and the pain will be worse than if he beats me senseless.

8.

Obsession is exhausting. We try to fight but that's what we've become. Obsessed. After one Sunday afternoon, when he fucks me seven times we make a half-hearted pact. We try for a while to spend as long as possible away from each other. It doesn't work that well.

V is a clever man. He knows how many hours or days I can stand before I become desperate, and he'll push that time just a little bit farther. A desperate woman will do anything, it's a fact. When my mind stops functioning rationally, my body takes command. Life is lived by instinct. Cravings have to be satisfied. Of course, I try to keep my feelings hidden. So instead, we play these silly games. I never ring him. I can't. I can't say, 'Come on over and fuck me, please.' I just can't. The exquisite torture I put myself through waiting for him to make the first move! And then he turns up on my doorstep with that dark, shivery smile, just at the moment when he guesses I'm about to boil over. Luckily, he's a good gambler. It's funny, we both play at being so civilized, him a respectable solicitor, me a teacher, but underneath we are both roaring like lions.

I don't know what's happening to me. I'm ashamed and proud of my sexual response. I thought only men felt lust. It's a word I'd never used seriously when talking about a woman. It's animal, it has no conscience. It craves, it hungers. Just like me. I do a little research with my woman friends. Some careful questioning. I feel I may have gone way over the top of the norm for my sex. I feel odd, a little out of things. There were a lot of women like me, on the fringe of the women's movement, allowing our consciousness to be raised but not being too radical. Where do I fit in now? Why do I have these feelings of unease about being disloyal to women? Why am I more loyal to a collective ideal than to the unabashed exploration of my own nature? I wish I could talk openly to my friends but I can't. I feel a little depressed. This kind of cruel sex is my sin, my guilty secret. I'm exploding with the energy of it everywhere. I know what Holly and Midge would say if I told them about V. I don't need to have them tell me I'm crazy. Midge was a battered wife. She left her husband, spent weeks in a refuge, had an awful time in court. Do I think she'll sanction this relationship I have with him? I must be crazy! So how can I enjoy the fact that V, in our sexual scenarios, raises his hand to me, spanks me, abases me, when I cannot square it with my friends? I tell myself I won't bring politics into sex. I won't allow it to crossover into the rest of my life. I'm not being used.

He won't oppress me, crush me. Will he?

I feel I've been slapped into life like a newborn baby. For the first time I know what it's like to breathe.

This morning on the mat are four letters. Letters from men I don't know who want to know me. I get a sudden feeling, a sudden rush that things might be going a little out of control. I'd forgotten all about the advertisement I'd placed in desperation months before I met V. I promised to answer them all. I have an uncomfortable vision of dozens of letters piling up. Having to concoct sincere replies. All that postage. So, what should I do? I could be callous and drop them in the bin. But instead I take them to college.

The staff room is empty when I take them out of my bag. I feel like a schoolgirl making a big thing out of an innocent meeting with the opposite sex. I blush. Who wouldn't want to get mail from so many eager men? I sit up, tell myself not to take it all seriously. I'll read the letters. I need some diversion from real life right now.

But these letters are about real life. Real desires for a relationship from lonely, bitter men. Men who've been rejected. I sympathize. I can pick out the anxiety behind the boldness. The writer is aware he will be one of many. He'll have competitors, rivals. Each tries to sell himself to me, trying not to offend, trying to accommodate every possible whim of mine. In other circumstances these men would be down at the pub commiserating, buying each other drinks. But not here, on the final meltdown of the white page. They're all like piranhas trying to bite each other, snapping for the prize. Me. And they haven't even seen me I think. I could be haggard and played out. They bite blindfold.

Trevor sends me a large photocopy of himself sitting on the bonnet of a fast sports car. It's been taken from an auto enthusiast's magazine. He wears a racing tee shirt, cool trousers and looks at me with such a predatory stare of smouldering readiness, so over-done, I almost laugh out loud. I fold him up carefully and put him back in the envelope.

The next is written in a tight, compressed hand. The letters are so small I have difficulty making out the words. I flick the page over and see the script is heavily embossed on the other side, puncturing the page in places. I squint and return to the content. It's long, rambling and bitter. His wife and son have left him. He misses them, he says. Over and over. I think he hates women. He grinds his suffering into the paper saying, please will I answer his letter. He's taken the trouble to write. Perhaps I will. I feel sorry for him. I felt much the same way myself, last February.

It's ironic but the letter-suitors don't mention the one thing they must miss the most. Sex. They think they're writing to an innocent Victorian flower. They don't refer to it. Yet couched in

131

every word it's there. I can give you a good screw. I'll screw you so well you won't want to leave me like my wife did. You'll see my prick and you'll become a slave to it.

No thanks. I'm already becoming one man's sexual slave.

Suddenly I feel depressed. I'm here in college. Zack's place. Suppose he heard us making love? I think grimly about the possibility for a while. But Zack's never the one to linger on the phone. He has a brusque way of slamming it down when the conversation is over. Me, I'm the one who listens to the click at the other end of the line before replacing my receiver. I get up and pace about the empty staff room. I'm tired of falling prey to thinking Zack is my conscience. Just because he owned seven years of my life—yes, that's what it feels like. And I'm trying to shake him off, still.

After my morning class I'm free. I have the afternoon to myself. Usually I go into town, to the library, or just to window shop. Today I want to be quiet. I walk from college through the park. It rained earlier this morning and now all the trees are sunk in a thick mist. Some are shadows, silhouettes against a milky backcloth. There's no wind. When I breathe it's like sucking water, not air, into my lungs. So, why am I trying to damp down this new sense of life within me? I'm almost unhappy about being happy. I laugh aloud at the thought. There's masochism for you! I think as I walk through the avenue of trees that this game with V will spill over into the rest of my life.

That's very scary. But then, I argue, isn't that what I want? What'll happen to me? I wish I knew.

I stop walking and kick at a pile of fallen beech leaf butterflies, all crinkly wings touched by flame. I stand there beneath the tree, calf deep in them. I feel different. Independent. Stronger. I'm a paradox. I pick up a handful of leaves and toss them in the air. Suppose it's him making me jump like a puppet, while he controls every string?

I don't see anyone as I go along. I wish I did. I want a friend or neighbor or student to interrupt my thoughts and talk to me. I want them to appear suddenly along the path I'm walking like a sign from God. They might unwittingly give me some great truths, cosmic revelations, the simple answers to my dilemmas. Just like that. The answers. Yes, this morning I'm ready to look for meanings in almost anything. It seems as though everyone else can make life's decisions but me. I fancy myself talking to the trees. They become philosophers. Here I am talking to the trees, asking for wisdom from the heartwood. When I was young I lay beneath a towering oak in July so I could look up through the perfect leaves, not yet spoiled by late summer blight, and call down the perfection. It was a sensation, I remember, of having all appetites completely filled; slightly crazy, almost drunk. Trees have that power. We have to lie at their feet to feel it. For a minute I shut my eyes to the nude branches around me now and bring back the moment years ago. I see the light fluttering with the leaves, coming down to me like diamonds.

I'm old enough now to know the trees have no answers, only the ones I give them. So I walk under the dying canopy of one, go to the trunk and run my fingers over the ridges. I walk in a circle, chanting under my breath. I put my arms around the trunk and hug it but I feel nothing. I feel a faint sense of disillusionment, of being spurned. Thrusting my hands deep into my pockets I stomp off childishly across the grass. I have my own values now, at last. I am working hard to erase the ones Zack gave me. They are the price for being married to him for seven years.

I get home feeling weary and restless. It seems too much trouble to think. I want to let others decide for me. It's easier to be led. I go upstairs, heave clutter into cupboards, throw myself down on the unmade bed with my boots on. Suddenly I get bitter, angry. I feel I'm being deceived, but I don't know by whom. I loathe myself. My mouth tastes of metal. I wish I could spit myself out and start again with everything simple. No involvement. I get up, strip off all my clothes and stare critically at my body in the mirror. I look at each part of me with immolate disgust. My body and I are not confident with each other. I feel a prurient voyeur. There are faint bruises on my buttocks. I am ashamed to look at them.

The doorbell rings loud and urgent. It's him! It must be! I flick the tears from my face and put on his silk dressing gown. I run down the stairs and

134

the hollowness becomes an ache I know he will fill. I fling open the door.

Zack stands in the doorway, legs apart, arms folded. It's his authority stance, the one he uses at the beginning of term to address new students. *I* know it conceals fear.

'I've got to talk to you.'

I smell alcohol on his breath and as I stand back he comes into the hall. He invades my home with his scent of after shave and deodorant. I feel awkward wearing only a thin dressing gown and I hover in the hall trying to decide whether or not to rush upstairs and dress. I don't like the way he walks about my living room looking at all the furniture and pictures as though it's all on loan to me by him. I decide to stay. He finishes his inspection and comes to a stop in front of me. Don't I get a kiss for old times' sake, he says? No. He laughs without mirth and sits down on the sofa. 'Ah, well, I never did have the right tricks up my sleeve, did I?' The fragile blueness of his eyes, the feature which once mesmerized me, glints like glass.

'What do you want?'

'Two things . . .' He holds up two fingers and waves them at me. I notice his shoulders shift under his jacket and I know he's about to say something big. '. . . I think it was a mistake.'

'What?'

'February. A mistake.'

The words fill me with a dullness as though I've heard of the death of someone close. New, sudden, not true. The breath in my lungs plummets

135

up, not down, held in check by the muscles of my throat. I am like a balloon, blown beyond itself, about to burst. Whatever I say will sound odd, rehearsed. Theatrical. I look at Zack. He's fiddling with the quicks on his fingernails. I wipe my hands slowly down the silk of V's dressing gown. Unconnected thoughts go through my mind. Stoically, in my new-found hedonism, I refuse to believe what he has said. I feel cold and remote. If I accept his words, I'm lost. But the slush of seven years is more obstinate than I realize and I find myself gulping back tears. Ridiculous sentimental tears. I make sure he doesn't see them. Harshly I ask about Carol.

'It's not working out as well as I thought,' he says, unable to look at me.

The sentiment vanishes to be replaced by bitter anger. Now, I tell him, just now when I'm getting my life together, he . . . I get incoherent for a minute while the anger rises and falls.

'I still feel responsible for you.'

I flee into the kitchen, slam cupboards, smash a cup in the sink, toy hysterically with knives in the drawer. When I return he starts to talk about the Byam Shaw on the wall. Do I remember why he bought it for me? That day, eight years ago?

Yes, I remember. A November day much like this, and we went to the Silent Pool. We climbed over a fence to get into the wood because officially the place was closed. The sparse clumps of grass and twigs underfoot were furred by frost. Dead twigs cracked and snapped loudly, advertising that we were trespassers. Through the bare trunks and then the pool flowing out of the trees as if it was not an entity in itself, but a glass eye, unseeing, open—in the winter face of a hibernating giant. The water is deep, some fifteen feet in the middle. Eerie, almost mystical, clear right to the bottom. The water has no secrets at all. Weed of a brilliant green grows vertical to the weak rays of winter sunlight. It's an illusion, this lake, a place for ancient saints to live their faith by walking across the surface. It makes you bend down and lay the flat of your hand gently on the water's skin to feel the wet suck on your fingers and rid yourself of the insane hope it might well be solid. Years ago a woman threw herself into the lake and drowned. Legend says she comes back sometimes to stare into the depths, thinking about the man she lost in love. I remember Zack telling me the story. He always had a way of making the past come alive. I can see it now; the trees all silvered at the edge in the dazzling bitter sunlight, the water all winking like crystals. It was a moment when I felt the pain of joy, never to be forgotten.

Now, my mind flicks through bright images of that day, her body rising up through the clearness, her hair and skirts floating out around her, the colors unspoilt, fresher somehow. Her fickle lover found her.

Zack says, do I think the past seven years count for nothing?

It's not him, or is it, that makes me sad? It's the place, a symbol of something gained but lost. Sadness for the future which then I could not know. For what might have been. Suddenly the memory invades and I lose my grip on the present.

I don't know how it happened. I choose to forget. It's over now and I lie back staring at the cobweb hanging down from the ceiling above my bed. Zack lies beside me. Our bodies don't touch. We are like commuters in a crowded train—close but distant, embarrassed by the other's humanness, no longer curious. I look straight ahead but out of the corner of my eye I see his hands clasped together on his chest outside the sheets. Little gobs of his semen slide down my thighs. I feel numb. I think it must have been his tears, the first I'd ever seen, which unzipped me.

I make a move to slide out of bed. He stops me with these words. 'That's how it should be done.' I don't believe I've heard them. I don't want to look at him, touch him—anything. I want him to go. I want to close my eyes, until I hear the front door slam behind him. He peers closer and says, 'The solicitor is dangerous.' A pause. 'Kinky and dangerous.' Is he talking about V? He is. My lips are glued. If I say anything my china jaw will crack. I'm afraid I overheard, he says. He's got one of these phones you can forget to disconnect. Maybe the little red light wasn't working. No. Maybe.

I hate them both. V and Zack. They play these games with me. They don't ask my permission. They score points. Zack has just notched up his score by a few thousand. So, what went on, he asks? I was crying, wasn't I? Begging . . . wasn't I? He slides down a bit under the bedclothes.

138

Words like cruel, depraved, pathological come smoothly from his lips.

I snigger. 'It wasn't real,' I say, 'It's a game.'

'Is it? What happens if it goes too far? What then, Rose?'

Zack sits up abruptly, compels me to look at him. There's something about his expression I don't like. It's more than the conceited zeal of telling me all he heard, all he imagined . . . He touches the inside of my thigh, slides across to me, his eyes shining. He turns on his side and his penis bounces against my hip.

I hit him across the face and yelp. He makes a grab for me as I fling off the covers on my side of the bed and jump out. He commands me to do things I've never done before in a voice I've never heard. Quickly, he raises himself on his knees and tries to reach me again as I move round the bed. I see the state of him, the size of him. I run out of the room, the hair on my back and neck on end. The dhurrie skids under my feet. In the bathroom I lock myself in and shout at him. I turn on all the taps so I cannot hear him moving about in the bedroom. Eventually the front door slams. I am busy directing the shower jet between my legs, trying to wash him away.

9.

I see V later that evening. He's got some crazy notion of making a video and is so turned on by the idea, he skips all the preliminary hellos and fucks me on the living room carpet within minutes of his arrival. I think about his prick all the time. I think of it banging its way up through me, attacking all the leftover molecules of Zack's sperm hiding in the folds of my vagina, and triumphantly filling my womb. When I come, I cry. It's the first time I've ever done that. Maybe I feel I don't deserve to climax. Maybe I wanted him to spank me first.

Afterwards he lies beside me looking in my eyes. He tries to read the open-book expression which floods my face when all the tension ebbs away. I wish he'd make some kind of definite contract between us. I wish he'd say something silly and possessive. I wouldn't have gone with

Zack, then. If I tell V he might punish me, forgive me. I'm having an impossible time trying to forgive myself. On the other hand, he might leave me.

I decide to go halfway. Test the water. I sit up, straighten my hair and move nearer to the fire. V is in the kitchen scat-singing and making tea. He's got a habit of doing this after he's fucked me. English tea. Symbol of civilization. He gets out the best bone china: cups, milk jug, sugar bowl. Sugar lumps with silver tongs. The small silver teapot which was a wedding present. When the tea is made he puts it all on a tray covered with a clean plain white tea towel. He brings it into the room. He feels like he's conquered something. Me. After the way we have sex it makes me laugh to see him pour tea. While he's busy I go to my bag and take out the letters I received from the unknown admirers. I have to start somewhere. I throw them on the sofa, wondering how he'll react. He sees them immediately. 'What's this?' he says. I explain and I feel myself going red. He won't take the lawyer's eyes from my face, but clicks his tongue and shakes his head slowly from side to side as if to say my case is hopeless. I stop talking and shuffle the letters together and give them to him.

He sits down cross-legged in front of the fire with his tea beside him and reads each one meticulously. I feel very awkward and ashamed of myself, although I haven't particularly, up to now. When he's finished he leans back clasping his

141

ankles and rocks back and forth. Well, he says.
Well.

I detect something in his eyes I don't want to
see and I get off the sofa and go to the French
windows. There's a strong wind blowing outside.
It gusts through the trees at the end of the garden
until the branches are almost horizontal and the
silvered trunk of next door's birch sways and
bows. It's raining leaves. Great flurries of them
come down and skitter about the patio like children's toffee papers. I turn and look at V. There's
jealousy in his eyes.

He asks if I've replied to any of the letters. Of
course not, I say. (How do I know you haven't
been seeing other girls, V, on the days I don't see
you?) He says quietly he hopes I haven't. 'Are
you jealous?' I ask. He smiles, gives a self-
deprecating snort and his eyes flicker. Yes, it's
crazy, but he does feel jealous.

I sit down on the sofa. I know I can't tell him
Zack fucked me. If he gets jealous over a few
letters, how would he react to *that* confession? I
shiver at the thought.

He runs his hand through his hair and his dark
eyes narrow. 'You have something else to tell
me?' he says.

I want to tell him everything. But I can't. Not
now. I hate the way he's looking at me. It's as if
he *knows*. I say I want to go out for a walk. There
is something I want him to know. I'll tell him as
we go along.

V gives me a curious tender look and gets up
off the floor, lifts my face and kisses me. I can't

142

take this unpredictable mixture of demonic sex and the gentle, self-indulgent way he treats me at other times. Tears slither down my face. He licks them up, threading his fingers through my hair, easing my head back and sweeping my hair from my face. Okay, he says, where shall we go? It's odd. Right now I don't want to have to make any choices. Now, he gives me a simple choice and I can't handle it. I want the macho V to come back, the decisive, slightly amused patronizing way he tells me what we're going to do. I don't want sympathy. I want to be slapped out of it.

I tell him I want to go somewhere torn, blistered, battered. I want to walk moody streets.

We go to the riot zone. Now, the roads are empty of chanting crowds and police clashes. There's nothing left but gutted shops cordoned off by railings and bulldozers behind the rubble. Everything on one side of the street for two hundred yards has gone. The smell of wet, charred timber hovers in the air.

'Zack heard,' I say, looking down at the dirty pavement and the leaves and litter in the gutter. I hear V sigh before I continue, 'He came round to see me.' V shifts his shoulders inside his coat, squaring up to the idea. 'What did he want?' he asks me carefully.

'He told me I was crazy seeing you.'

There is a pause. 'Is that all?' he says.

'. . . Yes.'

V looks at me. His eyes reflect the orange of a solitary street lamp. I am aware of him like a tiger under a velvet-collared coat. He stuffs both his hands deep into his pockets. His hair is as black as the black holes of the scarred shops behind him. The moist air settles on his curls. There is a long silence between us. I look into the city sky in the distance. It's split by colored rockets, showers of sparks and the sound of bangs like guns. They are celebrating Diwali. The festival of light. Us, here in the dark with my secret. At length I say, 'Are you angry?'

'Of course.' That little laugh again. Bitter, self-deprecatory.

'Are you angry with me?'

A pause. 'No,' he says. A sigh, long and drawn out. 'Not with you. What did he say?'

I tell him and he stops walking, takes his hands out of his pockets and holds my arms tightly, twisting them behind my back.

'You think I'm exploiting you?' he says.

'No. I didn't say that. He did.'

'Are you sure?'

I shake my head, trying to break free. When he holds me like this, with my hands pushed up between my shoulder blades, I feel he has complete control. I don't know if I like it sometimes.

'Tell me about sex with him.'

I ask him why he wants to know. He says, 'Shut up, tell me.'

I say I couldn't come, if that's what he means.

There is another pause. I can't make out his expression. Then he says, 'Go on,' in a silky voice which disturbs me, although I can't work out why.

'Sex was boring. Ordinary. I felt cold.'

'Cold?' He lets my arms drop and the blood

144

rushes back into the cold fingertips. I flex them in front of me deliberately.

'Yes. I always thought there should be more to it. Like passion.'

He nods and his breath pours into the night air. 'Oh yes. Passion. You like it with passion, eh?'

'Yes.' I feel suddenly very guilty about Zack.

He turns and treads on my toes. His lips are cruel. 'Passion, eh?' He is holding back something. Then, as quickly as it came, the uncharacteristic anger subsides. He gives an exasperated shrug and a sigh. A sly smile returns. All of a sudden he drops down to crouch at my feet. He flicks off his gloves and runs his warm hands up my leg underneath my skirt, deliberately scoring the skin, laddering the nylon. When he reaches the top of my stocking he stops. He slides his fingers beneath the suspenders, stretches them away from my thigh until I expect them to snap. Then he lets them go against my leg. It stings and I gasp, throw back my head. I have no choice how my body reacts to him. Why do I like it, I ask?

'Because you do,' he says.

He undoes the stocking, slips it down to my ankle and stands up, slapping his hands together. I stand there in the dark street. The light from the nearest street lamp fifty yards away glints and shines over black, wet, broken paving stones like orange foil. Rain falls now with more purpose. It fractures the surface, distorts the light so that it jumps away from its source, sharp and flickering. The nylon around my ankle is wet.

145

V pulls me out of the rain into a dark shop doorway. There are broken bottles and empty firework cases in the corner. The bottom of the door is charred. Small boys lighting fires. The hairdresser's shop is dark. The pleated blinds are pulled sloppily halfway down the windows on either side. 'Fix your stocking,' he says.

He is standing back in the deep shadows with only the white cuffs of his shirt standing out below his coat sleeve. I bend down and lift my skirt. Luckily it's a pleated one. I turn in towards him away from the road as a car splashes past. Light from the headlamps climbs the glass shop front and the dark cubicle where we are, and is gone. I am rolling the stocking up my leg about to fasten it when I freeze and look up at him. He leans back into the door, his ankles crossed. His head is bent and there is only the dark curls melting with the shadows. For a moment it's as if he has no face. He is a stranger, a voyeur, watching me with lowered eyes. He makes no sound, stays motionless. We are frozen like a sculpture. 'V—?' I say and my voice sounds weak, gobbled up by the silence made by the rain. Rain-silence. I pull the skirt up farther and the white band of thigh flashes for a second before I attach the front suspender and let the skirt fall into place. I hear him catch his breath.

His mouth is on my mouth and his hands are pulling at the buttons on my coat. Frantic, I look out into the street, at the black hole opposite which was once a supermarket. There are no eyes. No people hurrying down the road. If there were I'd

146

hear cursing as they tripped over the broken pavement.

I ought to say no to him. I can't. I ought to say I'm cold. It's raining. We're holed up in a smelly doorway like whore and punter. I deserve better than this. I ought to have comfort and schmaltz, everything just so. Music, food, consideration. Mollification for the Act. Rules. Etiquette. Courtesy. I'm a woman. I deserve these things! But V, he doesn't need anything, other than a glimpse of my thigh, the welt of my stocking, the little submissive jerk of my knee as I try to balance on one and a half feet, the lowering of my head. He just gives himself up to the moment. He's not like other men. He won't wine, dine, cosset for sex. He won't work out a little scheme whereby, at the end of the evening, I'll have *accepted* he'll fuck me. To him, that's a waste of time. No sport. No fun. It's like dribbling lust round the edge of a dinner plate, and watching it grow slowly cold in front of his eyes.

Yes, I ought to tell you, V. I ought to speak up for my sex. Women like it differently, don't they? We learn about sex life as an intellectual abstraction. We set up our own scenarios. Magazines. Journals. Agony Aunts. We are supposed to feel this . . . and this . . . The messages play on my mental screen one at a time, the letters big, childish. Not to be argued with. The same old stuff. But my mind isn't a sense and sex is. It's the only thing I have that kicks my brain into neutral.

It's a crucial moment for me. I see it all flash

147

before my eyes. How it ought to be. How it ought to be. And I feel my body telling me the truth. The plain non-verbal truth. As honest as the pain which is bound to follow when you prick your finger. My body says: I want it. My heart says: I want it. Thank God my mind is a million miles away from my genitals.

It's the suddenness, the noise he makes when he's fucking me, I find exciting. He moves in with a kind of cry as if he's found something he's been missing. As if in my body is the key to himself. He'll stop at nothing to get it. That cry is always there. I feel I am the elixir he must have to stay alive.

He cries now, like he's mad, in a rage, and slams his body against me, taking the breath from my lungs. Our coats are undone. He has flung his around me, shielding us from the road. A dark cloak. He forces me up against the glass on one side of the door, so hard, I think it'll break behind me and I'll go crashing through into the shop. The wet back of my coat squeaks on the surface like a rubber. He has my knickers in his fingers, pulling them down, cursing. I lift one leg then the other. Everything is wet, sticky, difficult. He is hissing with impatience. The heel of my shoe rips the gusset of the pants as I kick with my calf in an attempt to lose them. They hang round my ankle as I mount the glass opposite with my shoes. He won't wait, he won't. He pushes between my legs, lifting me higher with his chest, raising my buttocks, bursting inside me. I feel his nails dig deeply into the soft flesh between bottom and thigh. It's crazy. The coat slips away from me so we are no longer shielded. We have edged almost out of the doorway with the energy of our fucking. I turn my face up and find I am looking at the sky shot with rockets, the darkness, the rain falling silver through the loom of city lamps. It runs down my neck, my collar. I open my mouth and feel it hit my teeth. I bite it, bite the air, try to catch drops on my tongue. A car speeds past blasting reggae. I don't care. I feel my cunt growing ripe and soft like my mouth which is screaming . . . V slaps a hand over my lips. I bite his middle finger. He shunts himself far inside me, butting me with his head on my chest like he's compelling me to destruction. I feel him come and we make rain inside me. Everything goes slack. My legs feel as though they are made of cloth and they flop down onto the ground. He whips his hand between my legs and wipes his sperm on my cheeks. I am shaking. 'Okay,' he says shakily, 'Okay.'

At this time of night the Four Elms is almost empty. A few Irish laborers in the public bar have one before they go home. Two middle-aged office cleaners, their hair turbanned in scarves, have a quick gin before going to their work. The resident old black man, Toby, sits in a corner in his dapper suit, his grizzled hair and beard like trimmed wire-wool. The pub itself is half hidden between a toy factory and a row of terraced houses. The four elms are no more and if they ever existed in this concrete inner city sea, that flows right up to the red light spilling from the pub doorway, it's doubtful.

V takes my hand and we go down the side entrance to the lounge bar. It's empty. We sit there in the comfortable warmth, listening to the rise and fall of conversation coming through from the other bar. Later the room will be full. Country and western music will twang sentimentally from the juke box. There'll be drinking way past closing time.

The landlady makes polite conversation with V as he orders our drinks, her soft intimate Irish voice vaguely hypnotic to me sitting at the back of the room. It's timbre is like the rich red chairs and the heavy velour curtains, the wine red pile of the carpet, and the small, muted fox-and-hound prints on the walls. I feel warm, cocooned, and utterly relaxed.

V gives me my drink and slips my knickers out of his pocket and drops them in my lap. Quickly, I put them on and sit down again. We stare into each others eyes. The obsessive passion there is very near the surface. He kisses me slowly, doing obscene things with his tongue in my mouth. I want to tell him about Zack, but it would be like killing something beautiful to do it now. We have dizzy wheeling conversation like a joint monologue coming from our twinned subconscious. We talk about masochism. He tells me he's a sadist. I laugh. No, he says, that's what they'd call him. I ought not to laugh—I need him. How else would I get any satisfaction? I sit back. My hand rests on his thigh. If you're a sadist, I say, you need *me*. You can't be one all by yourself. So if people think sadists are cruel, that they have all the power, they've just misunderstood the whole relationship. They're not autonomous. Far from it. A sadist would hardly whip himself if he had no one to act as victim, would he? Yet a masochist can do that. I look at V. 'It sounds like equality of sorts, to me,' I say.

He scratches his head. 'You have done some thinking,' he says.

I slide my hand up to his crotch. 'I have power over you,' I say smugly. 'You say I need you, but you need me too.' I wriggle my bottom on the seat. I feel very good all of a sudden. I feel I'm on top. 'You only inflict pain according to how much I can take. If that's the case, don't I have the power? Who calls the tune? V—?'

I lean forward and look at his face. The smile on it has frozen. He didn't like that.

'Well, well,' he says. 'I can see I'll have to be different with you, Rosy.'

'Meaning?' I squeeze his thigh.

'We'll have to do something about this equality you talk of. I can't let you allow me to be dominant, can I? I'll simply have to push the boundaries a bit.'

'What?' I say, laughing. 'Are you asking permission? If I don't like it, then what? I might leave you. I don't think you can win.'

He sighs and slaps the table with his hand bringing the Irish landlady back into the bar. He gets up, buys another round of drinks and comes back to me with a dark frown on his face. 'Shut up, bitch,' he says. 'You're too sharp tonight.' Then the patronizing note in his voice comes back. 'I

151

don't mind. The stronger you are, the more training you need.'

I laugh, but he doesn't.

Oh, I say, that's a side of you I haven't seen then?

He gives me a dark look.

'No,' he says. 'That's to come.'

10.

We have been invited by Jasvir the grocer to the wedding of his only son. A traditional Sikh wedding. Vows. Commitment. Innocence. I don't want to go. V is very annoyed with my attitude. He takes me back to his flat and makes me think differently. His belt cuts into my flanks until I change my mind.

He wants me to wear Indian dress. Another cause of disagreement. Again his insistence wins out and I have to agree to the demand. He takes me to a tiny fashion shop in H— managed by two of Jasvir's daughters. He's turned on by the feel of satin, he says. He wants a kameez and churidar trousers, not the shalwar type—they're too loose. He wants to feel my thighs under tight satin.

There are rolls of satin along one wall and V scrutinizes them critically, pulling out several and unrolling meters of them, running his fingers up and down, holding the colors up to my face. I want one made for you specially, he says. I will give them your measurements. The satin, he adds in a whisper, feels like the lips of my cunt—slippery, delicious.

To help decide on the color V asks the daughter to let me try on some ready-made shalwar-kameez. He leaves me in the shop with the women and goes out. I spend half an hour in satin. One of the girls plaits my loose hair in a single rope down the center of my back. Apart from the color of my skin and hair, I look like them. They fuss and giggle and insist on dressing me, patting my arms and hips through the material.

These clothes are symbols. They are made to modestly hide the body but they draw attention to it. For me their experience is disturbingly sexual. Thin satin emphasises curves.

The kameez tunic is scooped at the neck, fitted over the breasts and shaped into the waist to fall loosely to the knees. The girls become quite absorbed. They choose a peacock blue costume with woven gold embroidery around the kameez hem, and drape a dupatta over my head and around my shoulders.

V returns, raises his eyebrows, says nothing. He looks at me as though I am a slave in a marketplace; nothing; not a woman but an object, dressed in clothes which emphasize submission. Ready to be bought, to be used.

There are two ceremonies and V insists we go to both. The civil one takes place in the morning

154

and we drive first to the bridegroom's house to follow the little procession to the Registry Office. We will go to both, V says, because I want you to learn a little about subjugation. He parks opposite the house. We get out of the car and stand there. He looks distinguished in his suit. Sexy. I wear a lilac kameez and tight satin trousers under my coat. Take your coat off, V says. I want to look at your body. His lips barely move as he speaks, and he doesn't look at me, but at the red door of the house of his friend. I shiver and wonder rebelliously why I am doing as he asks. Then the door opens, the groom nervously appears and stands in the doorway in his suit and red turban. He is painfully innocent and his face is fixed with an embarrassed smile. I feel sorry for him. Then— women everywhere, filling the hall behind him, making his young maleness suddenly frail, threatening to spill past him and carry his body out onto the pavement amidst the colorful tide of their costumes. The mother pours oil on each side of the doorstep. V bends to my ear and tells me patronizingly, as if I am an ignorant child, that it is a custom for keeping evil spirits away from the house and celebration. Pity I didn't have some charm to keep Zack out.

The groom is captured by the tide of women and pushed forward to a car decorated with tinsel and balloons. A man balancing a video camera on his shoulder pans the crowd. 'Smile,' V says through his teeth as the lens comes in our direction. 'They record everything. Ten hours of film.

155

You'll have to make sure you keep a smile on your face.'

We follow the family cars to the Registry Office where no one seems to know what to do and only V is at ease. The bride wears a red costume embroidered heavily with gold. She hangs her head and her face is hidden by the scarf which comes down over her forehead like a cowl.

'Part one,' V says. 'We come here out of courtesy. It livens up this afternoon. You'll have to do better than you're doing now, sweetheart.' Pause. 'Or I shall beat you. Okay?'

He insists on staying for the photographs afterwards, smiling, smiling. I feel angry with him. I want to leave.

He takes me to lunch in my lilac Indian dress, to an English restaurant where everyone stares. He treats me as though I am not there. I begin to feel I hate him. He won't let me drink but orders an orange and soda. He orders from the menu without consulting me. He tells me to go to the powder room and be a little heavier with my makeup. I want you painted on this occasion, he says. Asian women are always painted. He thinks artifice improves the natural beauty of a woman. Don't I think so? Use red lipstick, he says. Lots of it.

Afterwards he takes me back to his flat and tells me to change out of the lilac dress. He has the made-to-measure one he wants me to wear for the traditional ceremony. He insists on dressing me. There is a determined set to his mouth. His eyes are hard and shining.

156

The kameez is tight. The trousers tight. You'll wear the pants with nothing underneath, he says. 'You'll do it for me, won't you?' he says.

Pink satin slides up my bare legs and I feel thin pressure on my thighs. I am unseemly. He sits on the bed watching me and inserts a large white carnation in his jacket buttonhole.

'You need these,' he says, taking a pair of gold stiletto mules from a carrier. 'Put them on.' I feel selfconscious. I begin to plait my hair in front of the mirror and it all goes wrong. The silence between us niggles me.

Suddenly, he stands up, seizes my hair, and unravels the unequal sections. After making three perfect ones he brushes each carefully, draws the hair back from my ears and starts to plait. His face looks past mine into the mirror in front of us. His lips twist. There is more than a little cruelty in them right now.

The sensation of my hair being pulled and laced by him is enough to bring me to my knees. My scalp begins to prickle and the feeling goes down the whole of my body, amplified by the tiny rasp of satin against my skin. I am aware of every inch of fragile contact between us. Warm hands brush my shoulder blades and occasionally flick over my back above my waist as he works. My body grows toward his, asking for the heat from belly and below as he bumps gently against me and changes position. It sizzles there between us, never quite making full contact. I wonder if he knows what I am feeling.

I watch in the mirror as a frown of concentration

157

overtakes the smile. He stands back as the plait gets longer. The rhythm of his fingers tugs at my scalp and I want to curl up inside my silk skin. I smell him as I never have before. It seeps out from every pore, crying as if it had voice, into the silent room and the stillness between us. The plait drops now down the center of my back. It seems so heavy. It pushes against my spine, releases shocks of energy from the sacrum which shoot up. I am falling, falling down. As I go I catch a glimpse of myself in the glass. My mouth is an O.

I slide down his body as he turns me, knees giving way. Then the smell rising from him being pumped out by the collar, the smell of his hair, his neck. We sway against each other.

His fingers plunder the satin gently, lifting the kameez and slipping inside the trousers. As he reaches the smooth shaved dome of my pubis I am already coming. I squeeze my thighs together over his hand.

'Naughty.' He whips down the churidar trousers before they show damp. He tips me over his forearm, the flat of his hand on my bare stomach, flips up the back of the kameez, and brings the hairbrush savagely down across my naked buttocks five or six times. Before I cry out he jerks me upright and raises his forefinger in front of my face. 'Don't,' he says, 'don't cry. You'll mess your make up.' The tears are gasped back inside and I digest them.

Before we go he gives me a present. Gold and silver bracelets. I must wear the gold on my wrist,

158

the silver on my ankles. Thin twists of precious metals, linked together by tiny chains. Slave bangles.

We drive to the gurdwara. He leaves me immediately to join the men. Jasvir's daughters claim me and we go inside the temple together. We remove our shoes, and pull the wisps of our scarves over our heads. They tell me I look beautiful.

In the outer room rituals take place between the families. There are gifts of flower necklaces, blankets and money. V appears behind me and slides his hands down my back. 'Milni,' he says in my ear above the Punjabi din. 'The coming together of the clans. When we go inside the temple I shall be fucking you in my head.'

After a lengthy prayer everyone shuffles into the large room where the ceremony will take place. V takes a white handkerchief from his pocket, knots two corners and puts it on his head where it sits on his black curls. The floor here is covered with a white cloth. There are no chairs. A narrow strip of carpet leads from the door to the Granth Sahib, the Holy Book. It rests on a platform under a decorated canopy, bedded in a large quilt. The book itself is very large. To one side three musicians in grey turbans sit with their instruments between their legs, a tabla and two small harmoniums. On the walls are pictures of the ten gurus.

The men sit down on one side of the carpet divide, and we on the other. Immediately I feel uncomfortable in the cross-legged position. My bottom smarts under the cool satin. I find myself

159

blushing. Across the aisle V is watching me, serious, lids lowered. He knows what the sudden involuntary tightening of my cheek muscles means. Somehow he is more threatening sitting among all the men. They seem like warriors on whom we have to depend. The other women are happy but I feel slightly resentful at the enforced segregation.

The men walk up and throw money in front of the Granth Sahib before kneeling down and touching their foreheads to the floor. Santokh, the bridegroom, sits before them, rigid and nervous in his suit. I look at V and he makes me ache. I look at the boy's face. The innocence there hurts too. When the boy leaves the men and moves onto the cloth covered platform in front of the holy book, the wedding proper begins. I watch as the faltering bride walks slowly between V and I, leaning on two women who support her. She's legally married already, but it's this ceremony which really counts, which signifies their commitment of one life to another. Initiation proper. My initiation with V comes into my thoughts. His words, 'You owe me,' the massage, the sealing of his mouth to my sex to make his contract. I let Zack violate me without a murmur.

The bride is dressed from head to foot in red and gold. The dupatta covers her head. Here she is, supported by her woman, led to be offered like a sacrifice to the man. She sits by Santokh, hidden, like she is only a woman, not worth showing even her face. She rolls the frilled red edge of her kameez and pulls the dupatta further over her with gold-covered hands.

160

The granthi reads and speaks to them in a loud voice. Bride and groom stay silent, make no vows aloud. They promise in their hearts. Oh, V! . . . Bimla's father joins them symbolically by taking hold of the scarf which lies around the groom's neck and giving one end to her. There they are. Joined by a piece of cloth. The granthi chants the wedding song augmented by the musicians. Then the couple get up and walk slowly around the holy book, Bimla following her husband, holding on to the pink scarf. Cotton, a hairbrush, a belt, a hand striking the buttocks. The same. I cringe. Four times they circle the book making their silent vows.

I acknowledge silently too. What V has done has bound me to him more than any symbolic ceremony of submission could do.

And I broke the contract.

I feel like a whore.

The wedding is over. I catch sight of V looking across at me. The expression in his dark eyes is veiled, inscrutable. I feel he knows.

There is a party afterwards at a nearby hall. I try to hide my misery. It's hard to do so among the innocent happiness of the families. V sits with the men and drinks whisky. A bhangra group, friends of the family, make music and the men dance. They dance badly.

I sit honored, because I am white, by myself on the other side of the hall, not allowed to go into the kitchen with the women to fuss and talk,

161

and fiddle with the food. I feel isolated. All I can do is sit quietly, curl inward with my remorse and look at the men.

They move self-consciously in a circle, jerking their shoulders. Their smiles are fixed. They have not drunk enough yet to let all inhibitions slip. They flick their shoulders upwards as they shuffle—shy spectacles. Then the groom leaps onto the shoulders of his brother and the women clap, laugh, and huddle towards the men to dance in their own embarrassed clique. V dances with the men and looks at me. He beckons with his finger. Reluctantly I get up and sway with the women while the men circle around us. I am too aware of my body under the tight satin. It is now my shame.

Each time V passes me I receive the burning in his eyes. I cannot look at them. He knows, I'm sure he does.

11.

The white room at V's house scares me. The white seems to hunger for something else—the dark perhaps—the darkness in me which I am afraid of. Sometimes we are together in this room listening to music, and then I feel safe, untouched by this other thing. I can lose myself in music.

Sometimes he leaves me though, deliberately. He shuts the door and locks it from the outside. Then it becomes a cell, a padded cell.

I feel panic. I think of other instances in my life when this emotion has surfaced. I think of being trapped in a maze of neat, clipped, yew hedges. Impenetrable. The only way out is a paradox. I cannot see the entrance once I enter the maze, although in terms of distance, it's only a few feet behind me. No, I have to move towards the center through the confusing pathways. I am bluffed and cheated by false leads, sucked towards the unknown: the white seat under the cast iron gazebo. The terrible heart is a bluff. I arrive in a sweat, heart racing, to be mocked by this deceitful innocence, this illusory innocence where the exit through all the paths of menace is unbelievably clear-cut. And when I reach the little heart, I forget the journey of terror. I want to stay there. To go out is to have to return.

Lifts too. Alone in lifts. Boxes. No air. No freedom. Alone with myself.

It's like this in the white room. White. The dark part, the bit I'm afraid of is only myself.

One day he shuts me in with magazines, the kind *he* would read. He wondered, he told me later, how long it would take me to master my fear and allow my curiosity to open these forbidden pages.

My feelings toward V change. He plays a compulsive game with me, and I with him. I cannot stop responding to him the way I do, even though I am often angry with myself. More and more I want to be used by him, to give myself up as a sacrifice. This demon, this cruel love of his, the totality of it all. Is it what I want?

It is.

He tells me I will sit in the white room with nothing but my thoughts for as long as he wants. He gives me plenty of space to work out what I feel about him. No man before him has been this way. Other men have rushed me along, showed me their best sides but little of what lies underneath. It's been like drinking nothing but champagne, perpetually high on all the bubbles. No time to think, intentionally so. Snare first and let the deception slip out lamely afterwards. Yes, I've been like that with other men: a temporary actress away from the script and the subjective truth of my life, my Self.

But V, I've never known anyone like him. He is quite obstinately dedicated to let me experience all the darkness in his nature. When he beats me, he says, he's turned on by my tears. He's honest, I'll give him that.

But this behavior isn't a set piece, a little game in the sum of something bigger. It's not just an act within a play, no, but an expression of himself. There is no divorcing from the experience of his life. He has never apologized for its existence. Never felt ashamed.

I have tried hating him. The feeling has rebounded. I hate myself for even trying.

White room, virgin ground outside the window as the first heavy falls of snow come. I wake up at 3 a.m. in his bed. The thick red curtains are drawn and the room is in darkness. I feel the presence of snow. I wrap myself in the tapestry bedspread which I tease carefully from the bed. He is asleep, always that faint smile on his face as if he is amused by the cruelty of his dreams. I leave the bedroom and go out into the hall where the white stuns. The blinds to the living room window are up, and white from the blanketed garden flows up to meet the white carpet under my feet. It hurts my eyes and is wonderful. The black shapes, the shadow-side of snow-draped plants, and the stark-

165

ness of the furniture in the room sully the white untouchedness everywhere.

I sit huddled by the window slowly squeaking away at the condensation with my finger, feeling the cold breath at me through the glass. My mind is razor-sharp, running in all directions.

I turn and look at the black scratchy pen portraits on the wall. He displays pictures of naked girls being punished, where all can see them. When Holly or Midge come to my house I find myself shoving all my books under the sofa and slamming the ones on the bedside table in a drawer, in case one of my friends looks in. Has he no shame? It appears not.

V has knelt down silently beside me. I feel the heat of his breath on the back of my head. There is a fan of wet about my eyes and he bends forward, puts his thumbs on my cheeks and draws the wetness away. Are you laughing or crying he asks?

'Would it make a difference?'

'I think I prefer it when you cry.'

His black eyes. They have caught a little spot of snow-light underneath the pupils. The dazzling looks out from the dark.

'You are satanic,' I say, shivering with my laugh.

He laughs. 'Maybe. Maybe you make me so.' His fingers squeal down the wet window and he jabs them cold between my legs. 'Have you been naughty?' he says.

I shake my head.

'Good. I wouldn't like it at all if you had. I might have to tie you up.'

He takes my hand now and forces it down. Tell me, he says, how you do it. I want to know.'

My free arm is twisted high behind my back. For some reason now, I can't do this. With a new lover, yes, but the odd familiarity I have with him makes it embarrassing and difficult.

'Stay as you are,' he says. 'I want to get a torch so I can shine it at your cunt.'

When he returns, slotting batteries into a large silver torch, my hands haven't moved. One is still high up between my shoulder blades, the other between my legs.

'Do it,' he says.

He is like a scientist studying life under a microscope. When he lies down on the floor beside me he opens my legs and pushes the beam of the torch between my thighs. It looks surreal, he says. Your insides coming out to meet the world. How delicate. How I like to abuse you.

My fingers work away and I look down at myself, at the brilliant fuzz with an equal fascination.

See what you are, he says. Nothing but a cunt. What did I tell you? Now, you are a lucky woman. You know exactly what you are. Not many women do. What are you? Say it. A cunt.

He tells me as I come how I open like a pink, ravished flower.

12.

Classes at college are disrupted because of the weather. I video some programs for the students who do manage to come. V bribes me to borrow the video camera. He meets me outside the back college entrance. The snow comes almost to the top of his boots. We walk back with the equipment across the park, struggling and laughing with the black case and tripod.

He plays film director. I play out the various girls in his fantasies: the errant secretary, the black-stockinged sixth former. He eyes me, cold and remote, through the camera as if I mean nothing to him. He looks with a critical eye at what is spontaneous between us. I do not feel comfortable. He bruises the outside of my thigh because I have a miserable face on camera. I do not like the fact he will now have an instant replay on hand whenever he wants it—when I am not there.

Afterwards we sit together and watch the performance. I want to sit at the back row. I have first night nerves. The shock at seeing myself this way is too much for me. If necessary, he says, I will tape your eyes open. I will not have you feeling shame. Then you will be forced to watch yourself.

It is a silent movie, punctuated only by physical sounds . . . The sight of his face . . . The slight smile caught around perfect teeth . . . Eyes flicker with tiny currents of light, as dark as the space left by a blown-out candle. Legs, my legs, stocking seams not quite straight. I don't know what to do. I am waiting to be told. The camera lens whirs and grunts as he lifts up my skirt. Sharply now, over his knees, I turn my face away from the camera to avoid the deliberate ignominy of seeing red cheeks and nose inches from the carpet. The sound of his palm on my naked flesh thunders through my skull, throbbing with the pulse there, threatening to burst from my temples.

It is mechanical, this sudden obsession for detail—as though he is trying to capture something before it goes. I cry on film as his hand stings, smarts, on my bottom—not out of pain or humiliation, but because I sense change, finity, loss, and I do not know when it will come. I suspect it will be at my own hand.

'Harder,' I say, through my teeth, wanting him to crush these thoughts into anaesthesia.

I am angry, as I sit and we watch. Angry,

169

aroused, and almost in tears. Because he has made me beautiful.

V's demon is running a little out of control. Unknown to me he swaps the video of us for the one I have been taping for college. I do not know I carry an hour of uncensorable material in my bag as I walk along the slushy pavements. Carol, the flibbert, approaches me in the staff room. The video lies on the table in front of us. She asks what I have on the tape. I tell her it's a play about a black family living in London. A domestic drama. Carol wrinkles her nose but asks if she may combine her class with mine because of the low numbers. I watch her eyes and mouth. Her assertiveness ceases to bother me. I know she does not know about Zack's visit. I know she thinks everything is okay. My secret makes me smug and charitable. Okay, I say. Okay.

We walk together to the classroom. Her heels sound like pin-pricks on the floor, not stabs. She is taller than me but it means nothing.

In the classroom I set up the video and hand her the cassette while I leave the room for a minute to catch Ron Fennell as he goes past. I give him a hurried invitation to dinner.

Things are hotting up. The sight of my naked rear bent over a chair, and V pumping aggressively into me from behind, greets me on my return to the room. I rush to the set, widening my arms as I go in a futile attempt to block the screen from everyone's eyes.

Carol's mouth has sagged. She looks old,

170

shocked. She does not know what to do. I do not know what to do. A monstrous shiver goes down my spine. I want to be sick. Do they know it was me? Did they see my face? Do they know? . . . .

I snatch the video from the machine. I will have to talk to someone about this, I say, trying to fume, to set my shoulders high, trying to put acid stilettos in my voice. 'Wait here.' Without looking at any of the class, I walk between the ragged desks to the door, numb. V laughs when I tell him. He laughs so loud I could hit him. Why did you do this to me, I ask? I'm sorry, he says, 'It was a mistake.' But his eyelids flicker. They may have seen us. You. Me. I want our sex to be private, I say. I cannot bear to have others know what you do to me.

He corrects me. 'What *we* do.'

'I cannot tell even my closest woman friends.'

'Are you ashamed?'

'No.'

'I think you are.' A long pause. 'You are telling me what to do, Rosy.'

'No—'

'You say, don't do this. Don't do that. It embarrasses you. Oh dear.'

'I have a right—'

'No! Not with me!'

'I have no right to say what I feel?'

He shakes his head. 'No.'

'Why not?'

'I've told you before. I won't discuss it. This is the way it is. I'm not going to accommodate you.'

'And what about the rest of our relationship?'
'It may be negotiable. Sex isn't.'

This uneven mood between us. All churned up.
Like seeing rocks about to fall down on you and
being unable to do anything about it. The falling.
The splintering of a relationship.

The moment is before us. Coming on. It licks
up to us.

Now is the time to play my worst card.

The Fennells are coming for dinner. They are
making a special expedition through iced-up streets.
They must have something special, the works.
They must see me blooming, rid of Zack, leaving
the past behind. I am strong. It must show. Ron
will let stories of my new competence trickle back
to Zack. I hope he will feel punished when he
hears about me. He will know how much I have
gone on since that day. How easily I can forget
him, like showering his sperm from my thighs.

V is angry with me, I know it. He buys lots of
wine, opens the best, and starts drinking before
my colleague and his wife arrive. He does not
know when to stop. I slice potatoes and he pulls
down my knickers. Going down on his knees behind me, he pushes my legs apart and starts to
lick. His curls tickle. Please, I say. I won't be
finished in time. You'll make me late. He ignores
me. Growls. Laughs. I feel hysteria rise within
me. I am floundering, incompetent. I must do
things right. It must all be proper.

I turn to him, onion tears and real tears in my

eyes. V, I say. You don't know Zack came and I slept with him.

He blinks and looks at me for a moment before getting up.

'Aha.' Pause. 'I hope it was good.'

'How can you say that?'

He shrugs, licks his lips elaborately.

'Doesn't it bother you?'

Calmly he pulls me away from the sink and pushes me back against it again with his body, so I feel the edge of cold steel between two of my vertebrae. He takes my hair in one hand, wraps it tightly around his fist and jerks my head back and down.

'What bothers me, little one, is that you took so long to tell me,' he says in a low voice full of threat just under the surface. My hair begins to hurt cruelly.

'I want you to be angry with me,' I say. 'I don't think forgiveness should be cheap.'

Then I think about his last words and I feel a little faint. V smiles.

'He told me. Rang me up. Thought I'd bow out.' He pulls my hair so hard I mouth a scream. 'Surprised?' He chuckles. 'I must have been a pretty big threat to his ego.'

He knows. I feel crushed. Disillusioned.

'I had a nice time watching you be hard on yourself,' he says. 'If you'd told me. . . .'

'Why?'

He takes a piece of raw onion, chews it and licks his lips. Onion and cunt, he says. Delicious.

173

His eyes are like dark rods, satanic, piercing me. 'I'd have thrashed you. Made you bleed. Then forgotten all about it. You choose to suffer, Rose.'

Now watch yourself, V says twenty minutes later when the doorbell rings. 'Behave yourself.'

I rush upstairs to change into my dress: a small black, close-fitting plain affair. Fresh stockings. Too much trouble to get the seams straight. V won't let me wear tights. He went through my underwear and threw them in the bin—after he'd ritually scissored them into pieces.

Downstairs I hear his smooth, solicitor's voice. Nice to meet you. Charmed. She's just changing. A bit behind. . . .

The party is going ahead without me. I come down as black as my dress, wearing too much red lipstick.

Over dinner V tells them all about me. I am superwoman, a goddess, unbelievably wonderful. Dedicated to my students. An excellent cook. He is a lucky man. She decorated the house all by herself. What do you think of that? Just why did the husband leave? It's no way to treat a woman, is it?

Ron and Eva eat quickly, murmuring appreciation about the food. I know they want to go. Ron's face is red. He tries to speak and makes little puffing noises in his embarrassment. Eva drinks delicately, her glass always quivering at her mouth. She tilts it to be filled. She keeps pace with V.

V is splayed back in his chair, tie wrenched

loose, the two top buttons of his shirt undone. The glass waves in the air by his side like a question-mark. 'Isn't she sweet?' he says, looking at me, silent me.

V getting drunk, slapping Ron on his rigid shoulders. Winking at Eva. Come on—have some more wine, it's cold outside. Watching a middle-aged woman make a fool of herself. Aiding and abetting her. Ignoring me. Talking about me all the time. Ignoring me.

Ron, hey, Ron, you've got to put them in their place, eh? Need to watch them. Put up with their little moods. Put them in their place.

'Know what?' V leans towards Ron. 'I have discovered the secret. The cure.'

Ron looks across at me. I feel his hard brogue nudge my foot deliberately, in sympathy.

'I'm sure,' Ron says, after a minute's blowing and puffing, 'you treat Rosy very well.'

V is on his feet now. Eva bright-eyed. 'It's only fun,' he says, coming to where I sit and taking me by the wrist very tightly. 'Don't be silly.' He pulls me from my chair.

Eva, her glass tilted, some red wine dribbling onto the white damask tablecloth. Ron, frozen over the dregs in his coffee cup. V, sitting on his chair, back from the table, me, awkwardly ridiculous over his lap, the tops of my stockings, the white run of suspenders visible to my guests.

'You see, Ron, this is how it is. When she gets a bit confused, I just put her across my knees and spank her pretty little bottom. Like this. . . .'

Ron, Eva, shocked into their coats. Smiles stuck

their faces. So late. Didn't realize. Lovely time.
ye now. Bye. . . .

I wait until their car has crept down the snow-packed drive and onto the dark strip of the main street before I say anything.

'I do not need you,' I scream. 'How could you! My friends! You have gone too far this time!'

He grabs me by the upper arms, bruising them. He yells back at me. No, it's not far enough for *him*. It's all or nothing for *him*. I either agree to that now, to do whatever he wants, to submit, or he will go, for good.

I march to the door and fling it open.

He's gone now. Picked up his Italian shoes from under the table. Taken away his empty wine bottles. Wiped his feet childishly, symbolically, on my doormat. Driven away coldly in his silver car across the snow. Left me with red roses in bud on the kitchen windowsill.

The snow covers everything with its monotone of purity and there is no moon, no making of shadows.

13.

I want my freedom. I do. Freedom in chains.

I have acquiesced. Rung him. Said . . . whatever. He is cold, contractual. He won't come to me. I must go to him, this evening, in the cold, the dark. I must accept everything.

Freedom in chains. Outside it's dark, frightening. The wind sucks all the warmth from my body. I lumber through fresh snow in my boots, sinking up to my knees. There are houses all around me but I feel cut-off, remote, as though I am in an arctic wasteland. These home-people are shut in with their TV's, their warm fires and the light in their hallways, a talisman against the dark.

I want to cry. Why will he not fetch me in his silver car?

Among brown-stained snow tracks cars are askew. The snow there has hardened into patterns and shines under the street lamp orange like royal

177

icing on a cake. Snow puffs down my boots before I have left the drive and I feel my feet chill instantly. I find a tire track and walk along it, kicking the brown snow pattern with cold toes, rigid now inside stiff rubber boots. I need a chauffeur to take me to my reckoning. I need to feel *I* am making a special sacrifice, that *I* am special. The road plays hush-hush with the few cars that creep over it. V's car is not among them. The snow falls heavily now in the beams from the headlamps.

I wait at the bus-stop alone. The massive beech above me is bowed, cloaked in snow. Everything is closing down, ceasing. No buses will come, I know it. There's little point waiting.

The pavement has half an hour's fresh snow on the surface. It's hard to walk on it. I plunge in over the height of my boots into the drifts collecting in the gutters. I feel helpless, angry with V. It's only a bit of snow, I tell myself. But innocence has never looked more sinister.

The young birches outside the maisonettes are weighed down and the path through them blocked by drooping branches. V's door light is on in the dark. It's like a sanctuary.

So what happens if I back off now, go home? A life without V, without this ordeal? I know the answer. It would no longer work for me. Without him life would be an under exposed negative. A bunch of unscented flowers. Oranges with no color. Neither sun nor rain. No

minor chords. Tepid. Dusk. Hateless. Funless.
No cost or pain.

No feeling.

He takes his time coming to the door. He knows
it's me, hears my boots clattering against the
scraper, but he makes me wait. He ushers me in.
I glance at his unshaven face, not feeling it right
to meet his eyes like an equal. Because I'm that
no longer. He wears an old sweater with a hole
two thirds down the front. The ribbing at the neck
and waist is beginning to fray. His jeans are
patched. There are leather mules on his bare feet.
A smell of garlic on his breath. He guides, almost
pushes me into the front room, peeling my coat
off my shoulders as I go past. I see for a second
the disarray of magazines on the floor, cups on
the glass table, the dandelion paperweight sunk in
a hollow on the white sofa as if it has been thrown
there like a cannonball. And then darkness. My
eyes all wrapped up. Black cloth halfway up my
forehead, half way down my cheeks. Drawn tight.
The skin mid-cheek puckers in protest.

'Sit,' he says.

Without eyes, the normal actions of the rest of
the face feel grotesque, embarrassing, as though
they have no right to exist. It's not right to talk,
lick my lips, move a muscle. I am conscious of
incompleteness and that my mouth feels, not like
a mouth, but a split in my face, too mobile, too
apologetic. I keep it still.

He pulls off my gloves and puts a glass in my
hand. Campari. I like it even less now. I hear him
go to the French windows and stand there. I do

not know if he is looking at me. I sit on the edge of the sofa, fingering the crater under the paper-weight and wobbling my drink in the other hand. He is not so much looking as totally aware, even with his back to me. I knew he is. I can feel it.

'I hope you're wearing stockings,' he says suddenly, 'under that lot.'

I nod exaggeratedly and the drink spills onto my knees.

'Good. I want you to undress. Just down to your underwear, sweetie. Okay?'

I came because I wanted to. Now, I do not want. The rebellion against him sets in. I feel someone sit on the sofa next to me as I stand up, ready to tear off the cloth binding my eyes. I realize it is not V but another man. He takes my glass.

'Don't worry yourself, sweetie,' V says. 'Just get on with it, okay?'

The possibilities of what might happen if I do not do as V asks are dangerous to entertain. I take off my clothes slowly, stiffly. I am glad I cannot see the eyes of the man and be embarrassed by him. I thought I could play-act. I thought we were equals.

I stand in my underwear by the fire, blind-folded. If it were not for the other man I might have taken it off by now, peeped at V, grinned at him, apologized. The whole thing is stagey, a joke. . . . I'm sorry, truly I am. It won't happen again. The stranger brings a serious, slightly sinister note to the proceedings. I can hear my breath-ing—hardly there.

'We ought to have had some music for you to strip to,' V says drily.

'Can I take the blindfold off now?'

'No.'

I feel V come towards me, bringing coldness from the window. Then abruptly he goes away and the blinds descend with a crash. It is as if he has something in mind he doesn't want anyone outside to see. Something he is ashamed of. There is nothing so claustrophobic than my eyes behind the black cloth now, and the space behind the lids.

'I want to tell you about her,' V is saying. 'She is beautiful but a spoilt bitch. Yes, beautiful—her hair, wet by the snow, long, fair. Right now I know her eyes behind her mask are vulnerable and scared. She doesn't want to know what I know about her. She wonders what is going to happen. She thinks everything up to now has been a game, or perhaps *this* is the game. She's not sure. Her confidence is slipping. See, her lips are a little open, ready to receive. Pink, cold lips. She should paint them.

'I know every inch of her body. I've explored it with my fingers and my tongue. Imagine—my tongue—probing all her secret places. Places her eyes probably haven't even seen. But mine have. She tastes of musk, smells of clary. Odd, eh? She's embarrassed. See her hands twisting now. Her palms are sweating. She doesn't know where we are looking, what *use* we might be making of the various parts of her body . . . know what I mean? Let me tell you what the bitch does. When she thinks I might want to lick her between her

181

legs, she makes an excuse to go to the bathroom and wash herself there. She puts perfume on her pubic hair. I can't smell *her* at all. Then, innocently she returns, thinking she's outwitted me, that I didn't guess. She won't be so embarrassed when my tongue goes along and up in her clean cunt. Sometimes I kiss her afterwards. She doesn't like the taste of herself. She wants to spit it out. She turns her face away, saying the stubble on my chin is grazing her, but I know the reason. Bitch.

'Look at her legs. Very supple. She likes to wind them around my back when I fuck her from the front. She clings on there, won't let go, locks her ankles like a little marsupial. She thinks she has control that way. I feel her fingernails digging into my shoulders, scoring. Sometimes she makes me bleed. Bitch.

'Really I like to fuck her from behind, yes. I like her to kneel beside the bed or lie with her stomach on the bed and her pretty little rear sticking out. When I come into her that way she thinks I'm going to drive right through her. She doesn't like it much. I don't like that. I want her to be quiet, still, so I can appreciate the lines on her bottom. My handiwork. My drawings.

'She is disobedient. My disobedient bitch. She does not know her place, who she is or to whom she belongs. She belongs to me. She allowed another man to fuck her even though that relationship was over, and she belonged to me. And she kept quiet, didn't tell me until the time when she threw the confession at me like a weapon, because she

182

was angry with me. She thought I didn't know. But I knew. Bitch. . . .'

The other man is silent. For a moment I feel his presence is in my imagination, but then my ankle brushes against his outstretched trousered leg, and V is behind me, squeezing the flesh around my waist cruelly. My face burns with humiliation.

V continues. 'Until now she has never really known what I think, what I feel about her. She thinks I'm a nice guy, that I don't *really* have any nasty secrets. She's like all women. Like to think they have every man taped, catalogued. Think they can manipulate, maneuver their way in a relationship until they know exactly how the man will react, and what they can get away it. They stop being frightened. They lose respect.

'To me—I'll tell you—she's nothing actually but a cunt on two legs. An object I enjoy. I get a tremendous kick from beating her. If she cries, I don't feel sorry. I get turned on. It's appropriate: Woman restored to weakness. And it's not her place to be anything else. Not her function to make decisions. A cunt on two legs.'

His thumbs are at the corners of my mouth, stretching my lips thin and wide, baring my teeth as though I am a girl for sale in a marketplace, undergoing an inspection. I can smell him, the smell of his excitement, a certain brutality. Then he steps back and I hear him say the words.

'Do it.'

* * *

183

I have never been tied before. V often said it interested him. Now he watches me being tied by another man.

'Don't hurt her,' he says. I almost cry.

The man with no name, the cipher, compounder of my shame, is kneeling on the carpet in front of me. Soft rope snakes around my ankles and up my legs neatly through a series of knots.

'You want to be free right now?' V says. His tone is low, dangerous. I feel panic. No, not that feeling. Please. My insides are liquid. I am burning. It is as if my will has departed and a feeble butterfly flutters in my head. There are no more choices.

Knees pinned, thighs together, I topple. V holds me against him. The other man is expert, fast. I hear V murmur admiration.

'Why are you doing this?' I ask.

I can feel his smile. 'To free your mind, sweetheart. To make you aware of what you are.'

Soon my arms are pulled tight behind my back and forced up. If I move one part of my body, the others protest. All the time V is crooning, don't hurt her.

Thank you. A service performed for him by another. Together they arrange me carefully on the sofa and go out of the room into the kitchen.

Freedom in chains. That's what I wanted. I lie and for a while do nothing. I do not believe I am bound. There is no pain, no cutting in anywhere. Swaddled in rope. Made still like an infant. My mind cannot accept the condition. Then suddenly, childishly, I attempt to move all my muscles and limbs at once. Nothing. Straining against the swaddling. I hear the men in the hall, soft laughter. The man leaves. V goes into the bedroom and then back to me. The heat in the room increases.

I feel the slight roughness of flannel against my body. He is wearing his impeccable suit. The respectable solicitor. All convention.

'Open,' he says, turning me on my side and putting his thumb to my lips. 'Open.'

He slides into me, pumps, comes. I swallow. It is the only part of me I can move voluntarily. Never before. I feel no disgust. A kind of calm.

He carries me into the white room. I lie there on the white carpet while he lets out his demon until the skin of my buttocks is hot and pulsing. He tells me there are tiny red blushes on the wool pile of the rug. He gets ice and spreads it on my flanks. Red ice melting onto the white carpet. Pink snow.

He cuts the binding at my thighs and forces into me there. The violation goes on until he is exhausted. Then he lies still.

'Okay.' He is untying me and there is light, brilliant whiteness in front of my eyes. 'Okay. You're free. Get up now.' Our eyes meet for the first time. Some of the shadows in his are gone.

I can't. Can't move. I'm still there, bound, chained. Restrained.

Something has been transmuted from the physical to the emotional. I feel the soreness on my thighs but my hand won't go there to touch. Every function has stopped. I am a clean wiped slate,

185

needing education. Special education. I have lost part of myself. Refined, burnt away. A part I never needed.

He sits beside me now and smiles. The smile is innocent. Totally. Some of the old me comes back.

When will he set me free?

Will he?

Will I want to be?

What love is this?

The Boudoir
by
Anonymous

From the great tradition of *The Pearl* comes the unblushingly erotic periodical that shocked Victorian England – *The Boudoir*! Only six issues of this magazine were published and this American edition contains every line of the original numbers.

This compendium of classic erotic writing includes three complete novels – *The Three Chums: A Tale of London Everyday Life, Adventures and Amours of a Barmaid*, and *Voluptuous Confessions of a French Lady of Fashion*, and many hilarious stories, poems, gags, and informative tidbits.

The Boudoir is a delightful collection of the finest in Victorian underground literature. Circulating from hand to hand, this daring assortment of erotica was at one time enjoyed only behind closed doors. Now, at last, it can be read by all.

#6   ISBN– 0-929654-41-2 $7.95

The Sign of the Scorpion
(An Erotic Mystery)

by J. Gonzo Smith

"A whodunit so uncommonly exciting that the reader will not care who done it!"

Widely regarded as the best erotic mystery to emerge out of the 1930s, *The Sign of the Scorpion* is as enticing a thriller now as it was when first published.

Clara Reeves, a beautiful, inexperienced young girl of good family, is determined to find her sister, who has disappeared under mysterious and provocative circumstances. Clara's amateur sleuthing catapults her into a thrill-seeking world, and a labyrinth of sexuality. An attractive, rakish district attorney loses little time in seducing her, and under his expert guidance Clara's capacity for pleasure is brought to new heights. Ultimately, the dual worlds of her burning sexual life and investigative mission merge, providing a bizarre and startling conclusion.

$$\longleftrightarrow$$

He toyed with the whip while she bent over to pick up her panties, and touched her sharply on her bare buttocks with the stinging thong. "the Scorpion's sting," he suggested, as he watched the pink streaks spread and disappear on the young girl's sensitive behind.
Clara, turning to a mirror to fix her hair, stared at the sensual curl on her lips, as her flushed face regarded her from the glass, and wondered if she would like to feel the lash curl around her naked thighs in real ernest. It would depend on who did it, she decided, and found herself blushing scarlet at the thought.

#161 ISBN 1-56201-094-8 $7.95

BLUE MOON SELECTED TITLES

All books are $7.95 unless otherwise noted

Excess of Love – *Lenders*
An incredible tale of a dominant/submissive relationship between a man, his wife and their maid. #142 $6.95

Helen & Desire – *Trocchi*
The diary of a young g Australian girl coming of age in a small town during the 1940's. The novel portrays Helen as an intensely sexual girl who yearns for the outside world. #160

Eros: The Meaning of My Life – *Cadivec*
The true story of a Viennese schoolmistress who was a well-known advocate of corporal punishment to satisfy her erotic needs. #158

SM: The Last Taboo – *Greene*
A anthology of essays and fiction presenting the case *for* S&M. An original and provocative book. #157

Story of O – *Reage*
One of the all-time classics of erotic literature O describes the relationship between O and her lover and master, Rene. #130 $5.95

Beatrice – *Henden*
Probably the most sensuous novel ever to emerge from the Victorian years. #81

Frank & I – *Anonymous*
A classic first published in 1902. The narrator of the story meets a youth "Frank" and invites him home only to discover "he" is a young woman of surpassing charms. #02

The Correct Sadist –*Sellers*
An unusual book exploring the various scenarios that affect the Sadist and the Masochist. Beautifully presented and rich in poetic detail. #152

Love Lessons – *Manton*
Ten stories of amorous education drawn from suppressed chapters of Victorian erotica. #13

Sabine – *Vian*
A beautiful woman possessing an incredible aura of sexual magnetism embarks on a journey filled with frenzied sexuality. #29

MORE SELECTED TITLES

All books are $5.95 unless otherwise noted

___Algiers Tomorrow #127

___Amanda #131

___Beating the Wild Tattoo #132

___Birch Fever #140

___Bitch Witch #75 $7.95

___Blue Train #134

___Bombay Bound #42

___Brief Education #151 $7.95

___Captive #43 $7.95

___Captive II #98

___Captive IV #147

___Captive's Journey #141

___Carousel #34 $7.95

___Deep South #69

___Elaine Cox #56

___Ellen's Story #77 $7.95

___Encounter #78 $7.95

___English Education #25 $7.95

___English Odyssey #135

___Fantasy Line #9

___First Training #97

___The Hidden Gallery #121

___In a Mist #92

___Ironwood #22 $7.95

___Ironwood Revisited #46 $7.95

___Julia #164 $7.95

___Lament #153 $7.95

___Laura #112 $7.95

___La Vie Parisienne #9

___Mariska #65 $7.95

___Max #154 $6.95

___Merry Order of St. Bridget #120

___Mistress of Instruction #138

___My Secret Life #27 $9.95

___New Story of O #102

___Our Scene #41 $7.95

___Pleasure Beach #129

___Romance of Lust #116 $9.95

___Reckoning #32 $ 7.95

___Secret Talents #5 $7.95

___Shades of Singapore #146

___Shadow Lane #136

___Shadow Lane II #143

___Shadow Lane III #162 $7.95

___Shogun's Agent #49 $7.95

___Souvenirs From A Boarding School #159 $7.95

___Suburban Souls #12

___Sundancer #125 $7.95

___Tangerine #115

___Tessa: The Beckoning Breeze #145

___Transfer Point-Nice

___Tutor's Bride #30 $7.95

___Valentine #148

___Victorian Sampler #118

___Virtue's Rewards #101

___Women of Gion #36 $7.95

___What Love #117 $7.95

___Yakuza Perfume #119

BUY FIVE BOOKS GET ONE FREE!!

Bk #	Title	Qty.	Price
			FREE
	Postage & Handling		
	Total		

Name_____

Address_____

City_____ State_____ Zip_____

Check/Money Order_____ MC_____ VISA_____

Credit Card #_____ Exp. Date_____

To order:
Mail, call **1-800-535-0007** or fax **212-673-1039**.
Ask for our free complete catalog

Domestic– UPS; $4.00 1-3 bks; $4.50 4-6 bks; $5.00 7-10 bks
$.50 each additional book 1st class mail: $3.50 for 1-3 bks,
$.50 each additional book
Foreign – air mail: $6.50 1st bk; $1.00 each additional book.
No C.O.D. orders.

VISIT OUR WEBSITE! http://users.aol.com/specpress/index.html

Blue Moon Books
61 4th Avenue, New York, NY 10003
212-505-6880